ASSASSINATION OF THE PESHWA

A true story of sensational murders at Shaniwar Wada and the landmark trial by Ram Shastri Prabhune

Ankur Chaudhary

An imprint of
Srishti Publishers & Distributors

Srishti Publishers & Distributors
A unit of AJR Publishing LLP
212A, Peacock LaneShahpur Jat,
New Delhi – 110 049

editorial@srishtipublishers.com

First published by Bold,
an imprint of Srishti Publishers & Distributors in 2023

10 9 8 7 6 5 4 3 2 1

This is a work of non-fiction, based on the author's thorough research. Some events have been fictionalised for dramatic effect. While due care has been taken to verify all information at press time, any inadvertent miss brought to notice shall be updated in the subsequent editions.

Printed and bound in India

Dedicated to

Ram Shastri Prabhune,

the judge, who redefined justice.

Acknowledgements

I am fortunate to be born in India, a country which has a rich history and heritage. I am not a historian, but I like reading about Indian history. When I started reading about the Maratha empire, I was fascinated by it. It is just a coincidence that I live in Pune, the city which once had been the capital of the Maratha empire and a great place to be in if you are interested in Maratha history.

During the research for this book, I read about many powerful and visionary leaders of the time who impressed me, but I was particularly captivated by the life of Madhavrao Peshwa. He was the fourth Peshwa from Bhat family and had qualities of both his father, Nanasaheb Peshwa, and his grandfather, Bajirao Peshwa. He was not only a fierce warrior, but also an astute politician.

It was during the reign of Madhavrao Peshwa that Ram Shastri Prabhune became Chief Justice of the Maratha empire. You will learn more about him when you read the story.

This book would not have even existed without the guidance of my literary agent Suhail Mathur from The Book Bakers literary agency. It was during a casual conversation when Suhail suggested me to write a book about Ram Shastri Prabhune. I delved deep into the Maratha history and when I finally decided to take this story to the readers, Suhail was a constant support during the writing journey.

Namrata, from Keemiya Creatives, supported me in proof reading and editing the story in the early stages and her contribution helped in shaping up the story.

I am thankful to my editor Stuti Gupta and my publishing team at Srishti Publishers led by Arup Bose for picking this story and bringing it to life. They believed in this story and have been very supportive and encouraging on this journey.

I am thankful to numerous historians and authors who had researched and written extensively about the Maratha empire. Their work has been a great source of information and inspiration in writing this book.

I dedicate this book to my family. Varuna, my wife, who always supports me while I spend countless hours reading and writing stories. Anaya, my inquisitive daughter, who keeps asking many intriguing questions about the Peshwas, Shivaji Maharaj and the Maratha empire. Ved, my son, who is too young to understand any of this, but still loves to sit on my lap and stare at the laptop while I write.

At last, to my readers. I am thankful to you for choosing this story. Hope you will enjoy reading it as much as I enjoyed writing it.

1 THE JUDGEMENT DAY

October 1773
Maratha Darbar, Alegaon

The night in Alegaon was buzzing with political activity. One could hear the footfalls of the soldiers walking, palanquin bearers arriving and the clopping of horses as the guests were pouring in from all corners of the Maratha empire. Alegaon had turned into a big Maratha camp over the last few weeks. Anandibai was in the darbar, standing in front of the *musnud,* and staring at it. The guards were standing some distance away from her with *mashaal* in their hands to lighten the darbar for her. For the last few days, she had been taking care of all the preparations for the coronation of her husband as the next Peshwa of the Maratha empire.

'This darbar will witness history in a few days,' thought Anandibai. She heard someone approaching her and turned around to see that her *dasi* had arrived for the fourth time that evening. Anandibai understood that it was very late in the night.

"I know you want me to take rest now, but I will not get any rest till *Swari* becomes Peshwa." Anandibai chuckled and signalled her dasi and guards to follow her. As she came out of the darbar, guards quickly walked in front of her to show her the path in the dark. She reached her chamber, confident of the preparations. Everything had gone as per plan, except for one thing.

'*Will Ram Shastri come?*' a question crossed her mind. It was going to be a long night for her in Alegaon.

* * *

It was a quiet night in Poona and the weather was pleasant due to the onset of the winter season. All the windows and doors of his house were closed and no mashaal or *diya* was lighted inside. Ram Shastri wanted to remain in the darkness; darkness which many in the empire had already embraced. The moon was already up in the sky, shining in the darkness of the night and giving him some hope in darker times. The invitation to join the coronation ceremony was lying next to him with a special mention of his name as the distinguished guest.

Ram Shastri had joined the Maratha empire as a clerk more than two decades back, during the reign of Nanasaheb Peshwa. With his knowledge, hard work and devotion, he rose through the ranks to become the Chief Justice of the empire. In his tenure as the Chief Justice, he had never hesitated in delivering difficult decisions in the darbar. It was for the first time in his life that he was contemplating his options.

It was a long night for Ram Shastri too. The opportunity had finally arrived when he could deliver justice to the most tragic and sinful incident that Marathas had ever witnessed. He spent the whole night contemplating the ramifications that the judgement could have on the affairs of the state, along with the danger it could bring to him and his family. He was unfazed by the threats and resistance he had faced during the investigation.

The Maratha empire was in turmoil for the last few weeks and Ram Shastri was well aware of the consequences of the judgement. The succession dispute could lead to a political crisis, which would only get worse with his judgement.

'Should I postpone the delivery of the judgement for the sake of political continuity and stability?' thought Ram Shastri. He did not realize when he dozed off, till the chants of Ganpati aarti from a nearby temple woke him up. As the dawn broke, with the arrival of sunlight, the darkness slowly disappeared from his house. A new day had started, but it brought no respite for him. Ram Shastri was still not able to make up his mind.

Maratha empire was buzzing with a political activity that was never seen before. There were rumours, conspiracies, and a strange fear of the unknown. Subjects were talking in hushed tones inside their houses, traders were discussing this in the *bazaars*, and officials were talking at their workplaces. Everyone in the city had only one question on their minds – *'Is it true?'*

In that year, it was relatively peaceful in most parts of the continent. There had not been much political activity and, for the last few months, the focus of Hindustan had shifted to Poona. Maratha Chiefs, loyalists, friends and enemies were keenly observing the happenings at Shaniwar Wada, and the public at Poona was concerned about the way power had shifted in the last few months. *'Are we forgetting the moral values which were taught to us by Chhatrapati Shivaji Maharaj?'* questioned many in the empire.

* * *

"You look tired today," Janaki exclaimed as she walked towards the prayer room with a thali of aarti in her hands.

"Join me for the morning aarti," Janaki said again as she did not get any response from him.

Ram Shastri had finished his morning rituals and had joined his wife in the prayer room, however, he did not respond to the question asked by Janaki. Once the aarti was over, he took the blessings of Lord Ganesh and Janaki offered him the *prasada.*

Janaki was looking at her husband. The breakfast served to him was untouched and he was lost in thoughts.

"Gajanan will answer our prayers," said Janaki. Ram Shastri did not respond again and silently started munching his breakfast.

The coronation of Raghunathrao was just two days away and the city of Poona was celebrating, rather forcefully. All the houses were thoroughly checked by the soldiers and owners were heckled if they did not find the *toran* adorning the entrance. As the guards approached Ram Shastri's house, they found no toran and no decoration. The soldiers rushed and invited their leader as they were excited to find a house without toran. The leader of the group arrived on the horse and as he got down from his horse in front of the house, he realized that this was the house of the Chief Justice of the Maratha empire.

"*Hujur*, what are you thinking? We should ask the owner to come outside immediately," said a soldier in the group.

"Let me fetch a toran from a nearby house," said another soldier and rushed away. Slowly, a few more soldiers arrived on their horses as they were happy with another opportunity to exercise their power.

"Let me pull the owner from inside," a soldier came forward

and rushed towards the gate.

"Stop! Do you have an idea who stays here?"The leader was agitated. He was still in two minds. Ram Shastri had a stature in the Maratha empire and had been a senior member under previous Peshwas.

The group of soldiers was getting impatient with the inaction of their leader. The soldiers were waiting for some entertainment and the crowd started gathering outside the house of Ram Shastri.

A soldier had already fetched a toran and started putting it at the entrance of the house; the crowd started cheering in anticipation.

"Long live Shrimant Raghunathrao Peshwa," shouted the group of soldiers.

Ram Shastri and Janaki heard the noises coming from outside and for a while, they ignored thinking that it would be a group of soldiers roaming around the city.

"Do you hear these noises?" asked Ram Shastri and Janaki nodded.

"I will go and check." Janaki walked towards the door.

"Oh, Lord!" Janaki exclaimed as soon as she opened the door. When she saw the crowd outside, she immediately closed it and rushed inside.

"What happened?" Ram Shastri asked her. Her facial expressions conveyed that something was wrong.

The crowd, which was looking with anticipation as the door of Ram Shastri's house opened and he emerged from inside, shouted in his favour. He looked around and was surprised to see a gathering of people and some Peshwa soldiers outside his house.

A soldier who was putting the toran at the entrance lost his balance and one side of the toran fell on Ram Shastri's head, it was then he grasped the reason for the gathering and lost his cool.

"Stop it now and get away from my house!"Ram Shastri said authoritatively and pulled the toran.

"Shastribuwa, the empire is in a celebratory mood and it is the order of Shrimant Raghunathrao Peshwa that all the houses should be decorated," the leader responded.

"Dadasaheb is yet to become Peshwa. I order you to remove this and get away immediately," Ram Shastri stood firm. Fearing the consequences of fighting with the judge of the empire, the soldiers stepped back. The leader of the group warned Ram Shastri of the consequences for having defied the order of the Peshwa and left. Soon, the crowd also dispersed.

"Why are you so angry with these soldiers? They are just following orders," Janaki asked, Ram Shastri did not respond. With a heavy heart, he decided to get ready and leave for Alegaon.

"You are angry with these soldiers here, but going to join the coronation ceremony in Alegaon!" Janaki said sarcastically.

"I have decided to go to Alegaon, but I am still not sure about the purpose of my visit," Ram Shastri responded.

"Have you forgotten the promise you made to Shrimant Madhavrao Peshwa on his death bed? Do you remember the face of Vahinisaheb when she visited you a few days back?" Janaki questioned him again.

"I have not forgotten anything, Janaki! But how can I fight this battle alone? What happened that day in Shaniwar Wada is an open fact now. However, instead of focusing on getting justice for the deceased Peshwa, the whole Maratha empire is eagerly waiting for the coronation of the new Peshwa," Ram Shastri's voice quavered.

"It is the responsibility of the Chief Justice of this empire to deliver justice and show the right path to everyone. If not you, then who will?" Janaki said calmly.

"What should I do Janaki?"Ram Shastri stared into oblivion, unsure whether the question he asked was for Janaki or himself.

Ram Shastri had never felt so helpless in his life. In the past, on many occasions, he had stood in the darbar and questioned the decisions of Madhavrao Peshwa. That was the time when a judge commanded immense respect in the Maratha court. He even had the authority to question the Peshwa, but times had changed.

"I am unable to see a way out of this situation Janaki. What should I do?" he repeated his question.

"Something that you have always done!" Janaki said and added, "Justice!"

She looked at her husband with pride in her eyes. Ram Shastri was ready to leave for Alegaon; he was already late and the *palki* was waiting for him outside his house. Ram Shastri walked towards the door and Janaki followed him.

Before boarding the palki, Ram Shastri turned back and looked towards Janaki. He waited for a while before speaking, weighing his words.

"Do you know the cost of justice, Janaki? I don't think it is any safer in the empire to deliver justice. You have seen what happened just now," Ram Shastri was concerned. Janaki could sense the fear in her husband's voice.

"The path of truth and justice has always been dangerous, but in the end, you come out victorious. You have the proof and truth on your side and the blessings of Gajanan. God is giving you a chance to uphold the values of Shivaji Maharaj," Janaki tried her best to motivate him.

Ram Shastri boarded the palki. It was a long journey ahead and on his way, he thought about the discussion he had with Janaki. The last few months had been very cruel in Shaniwar Wada which had seen conspiracies, rebellion, deceptions and murders. Ram Shastri took it upon himself to investigate the murders against the wishes of many in the empire and he had taken the investigation to a logical end.

It was time for the judgement!

By the time he reached Alegaon, it was late in the night. Ram Shastri had not informed anyone about his arrival to keep it a secret till the day of coronation. It was important to protect the proof and stay out of political influence. Ram Shastri also needed time to make up his mind and had decided not to meet even Nana Phadnis and Haripant Phadke, who were already camping in Alegaon.

On the morning of the coronation day, Ram Shastri sent a message to Raghunathrao about his arrival in Alegaon. Raghunathrao was happy that his coronation would have the formal approval of the Chief Justice.

All the dignitaries were captivated by the grandeur of the venue of coronation, which looked like a replica of Ganpati Rang Mahal at Poona. The darbar was buzzing with activity, all the dignitaries were pouring in, wishing each other and taking their respective seats.

"To all present in the darbar, Shrimant Raghunathrao Peshwa is arriving," announced a guard. Raghunathrao had taken a ride of the area and had arrived on an elephant. As he entered the darbar, everyone rose to pay respect to the new Peshwa.

Raghunathrao greeted everyone and slowly walked towards the musnud.

"Where is Shastribuwa?" Raghunathrao asked Visajipant. He was upset to see that Ram Shastri had still not arrived.

"He has still not arrived in the darbar, Shrimant," replied Visajipant Lele.

It was a tradition that the Chief Justice of the Maratha empire walks the new Peshwa to the throne and officially declares him the next Peshwa.

"I can see that. I order you to immediately go and check on Shastribuwa," Raghunathrao said irritatingly and looked towards Anandibai. She signalled him to take the musnud.

"Stop Visajipant!" Raghunathrao called Visajipant who had turned to leave the darbar in search of Ram Shastri.

"Sarkar!" Visajipant looked puzzled. Raghunathrao signalled with his hand and Visajipant immediately understood the gesture and together they started walking towards the musnud. They had walked a few steps only when Ram Shastri arrived.

"Stop Dadasaheb!" Ram Shastri ordered from the other end. The dignitaries present were a bit surprised by his tone. There were murmurs in the darbar.

Ram Shastri looked around the darbar, slightly bent his head to pay his respect to all the dignitaries, and slowly started walking towards Raghunathrao.

Sumer Singh was in-charge of security for the coronation and Gardis were present in all corners of the darbar. Sakharam Bapu and Nana Phadnis were there, along with other ministers.

Mahadji Scindia and Tukoji Holkar were also present, as were other imminent Maratha Chiefs. It was difficult for Ram Shastri to gauge the mood of the darbar.

Ram Shastri scanned all the faces to check who could support him in delivering the judgement and facing its immediate consequences.

"Dadasaheb, do you still consider me the Chief Justice of the Maratha empire?"Ram Shastri asked Raghunathrao, bent in front of him, and did a respectful salute.

"Shastribuwa, we waited for you for so long. Why are you late for the ceremony?" Raghunathrao asked politely as he sensed that Ram Shastri was unhappy that the coronation ceremony had started without him.

"I had some urgent work, Dadasaheb!" Ram Shastri replied diplomatically.

"What could be more urgent than this, Shastribuwa?" Raghunathrao hinted towards the full darbar and dignitaries who had gathered for the ceremony.

Ram Shastri bowed again and apologized to everyone in the darbar with folded hands.

"Shastribuwa, you are and will remain the Chief Justice of Marathas. My sword will always protect you. Now I request you to perform your duty," Raghunathrao requested Ram Shastri to walk him to the musnud.

Beautiful petals of marigold flowers were showered on Raghunathrao by dasis from the second floor, where Anandibai was sitting and proudly observing her husband's coronation as Peshwa.

'*Why is he doing all this drama? I had worked so hard for years for this day and now* Ram Shastri *is here,*' thought a concerned Anandibai, who was still worried about the sudden arrival of Ram Shastri.

Anandibai looked towards Sumer Singh and signalled him to be ready. Sumer Singh, slightly bowed his head towards her with one hand on his sword, conveying that he was ready to tackle any difficult situation that could arise. Anandibai nodded with a smile on her face.

"Thank you Dadasaheb for showing your love and respect for me and bestowing upon me this great responsibility. As the Chief Justice of this court, I feel honoured to walk the next Peshwa to the musnud." Ram Shastri declared and both of them started walking.

This was the moment all the dignitaries present had been waiting for. This was the moment Ram Shastri too was waiting for.

"What happened Shastribuwa?" Raghunathrao asked Ram Shastri, who had stopped just a few steps before the musnud.

"You have asked me to perform my duty Dadasaheb and that is the main reason why I am here in this darbar today – to perform my duty to this throne of the Marathas. Shrimant Narayanrao Peshwa was murdered two months back at Shaniwar Wada and we could not find the culprit. The Peshwa gets murdered at his palace and we don't know who is behind his murder, and we all have conveniently forgotten about it. There are many dignitaries present in this court who want to ensure that there should not be any political crisis that could harm the interest of the empire. This seat of Marathas, this musnud, should not remain empty. That is a political issue, but I am not a politician. I am the judge of this empire and my primary duty is not to ensure the political continuity of the empire. My primary duty is to deliver justice for the people of the empire."

"Shastribuwa, I also feel the loss of Narayan and I agree with you that justice should be delivered. Our Narayan should get justice." Raghunathrao tried to bluff Ram Shastri, his lips were trembling and his hands were sweating.

"Dadasaheb, delivering justice is my duty and today, I am going to perform my duty with utmost honesty and integrity."Ram Shastri surprised everyone in the darbar with his announcement.

"I have investigated the murder of Shrimant Narayanrao Peshwa and today in front of this darbar I would deliver my judgement," he continued.

Ram Shastri again looked at all the dignitaries present in the darbar. Most of them were clueless about what Ram Shastri was up to. Raghunathrao, who was irritated by the sudden announcement, was getting jittery as he had no idea about the progress of the investigation. Anandibai was stunned by the announcement Ram Shastri had just made. '*It is not a good sign,*' she thought.

With watery eyes, Ram Shastri bent to pay respect to the musnud, which was empty at that time, and got ready to announce the judgement on the most tragic incident in the history of the Maratha empire.

PANIPAT – THE BEGINNING OF A DISPUTE

2

March 1760
Shaniwar Wada, Poona

The Mughal Empire was on a decline in the early eighteenth century. The last decade or so had seen constant infighting to capture Delhi. The fall of the Mughals was an opportunity for the Marathas, who rose to prominence under Bajirao Peshwa and expanded the empire in the north and south. When the Marathas were expanding the empire in the Indian subcontinent, Nader Shah was expanding his kingdom from Iran to Afghanistan and slowly, was advancing towards Delhi.

In the battle of Karnal in the year 1739, Nader Shah allied with Nizam of Hyderabad and defeated the Mughals to capture Delhi. Nader Shah tortured the populace, looted and destroyed the beautiful city. After the assassination of Nader Shah, Ahmad Shah Abdali from Afghanistan took charge of the empire. Ahmad Shah Abdali had invaded Hindustan four times and was planning another campaign to Delhi as the Marathas had become a constant threat to the existence of Mughals and other Muslim rulers in India. They were concerned about the rise of a powerful Hindu empire.

Abdali was seen as a savior by these rulers and they requested him to protect the Mughals and other Muslims of India. Najib

Khan, who was an ally of the Marathas, but later defected, wrote to Ahmad Shah Abdali to come to Delhi and fight the Marathas.

The Maratha darbar was discussing the plan to counter the rise of Ahmad Shah Abdali in Delhi. Najib Khan had switched sides and allied with Ahmad Shah, who supported him to take the post of Mir Baksh in Mughal darbar. Najib Khan was effectively running the Mughal empire from Delhi after switching the camps from Marathas to Mughals.

"We have to take care of Najib Khan first; he could prove to be dangerous. We all know that he is the one who sought help from Ahmad Shah and invited him to Delhi. That snake must be crushed and then we can march further north to counter Ahmad Shah," Sadashiv Bhau told the darbar.

"The bigger concern right now is Ahmad Shah. He had to be stopped this time. We all know that he has plans to come to Delhi again. His intentions are clearly to confront us and stop the expansion of the Maratha empire," said Nanasaheb Peshwa sharing his thoughts with the darbar after much deliberation.

"In that case, we should immediately plan a campaign in the north. Ahmad Shah is not far away from Delhi and he is coming with a large army this time," Sadashiv Bhau sounded agitated.

"Yes, we must make preparations to send our army to the north at the earliest to stop Ahmad Shah this time. We should send a clear message to the world – Hindustan will not tolerate invaders now," Nanasaheb said with anger in his voice.

"We are in a difficult financial situation and to fight Ahmad Shah, we need a large army which will come at a very high cost," Raghunathrao shared the harsh reality of the treasury with everyone in the darbar.

"I am well aware of our financial situation Raghunathrao," Nanasaheb said sadly and coughed violently for a while. His health had been deteriorating for many months and the consistent cough had made him weaker.

"We need resources to fight against mighty Ahmad Shah," Raghunathrao said cunningly.

"You have fought many battles in north Raghunathrao, and know the territory well. What should be our best strategy to counter Ahmad Shah?" Nanasaheb asked in a terse tone. He was not happy that his brother was appreciating the enemy in a full darbar.

"We have to stop Ahmad Shah from reaching Delhi. If he reaches Delhi, then he will have the strong support of local Mughal and Muslim allies. We should stop him near Lahore," responded Raghunathrao, recognizing the discomfort in Peshwa's statement.

Raghunathrao had been the most successful Maratha commander in the north for many years during the reign of Nanasaheb. He had single-handedly taken the Maratha flag up north till Lahore. Nanasaheb trusted the war tactics of his younger brother who had proven himself on the battlefield.

"If you have to go on a campaign to the north to counter Ahmad Shah, what resources will you need?" Nanasaheb knew that Raghunathrao was the most suited commander to take on Ahmad Shah.

"I will be proud to lead this campaign and I think we can easily defeat him. For this campaign, I will need a contingent of eighty thousand soldiers and fifty-five lakh rupees," Raghunathrao told Nanasaheb.

Nanasaheb could not speak for a while. He coughed again when he heard the demands of his brother, slightly changed his position in his seat and looked around the darbar. Everyone was silent. Sadashiv Bhau wanted to speak, but Nanasaheb signalled him to stop.

"You are aware of the financial debts, Raghunathrao. We don't have that much money in the treasury. You have to garner some support from our northern allies."

"I will take support in the north also, but unfortunately, our two key allies in the north, Holkar and Scindia, are not on good terms with each other. I think it would be difficult to convince both of them. I am also concerned about the support from Rajputs and Jats. Many of our northern allies may not go against Ahmad Shah."

"Shrimant, even if we get some support in the north, we don't have that much money in the treasury to afford that kind of campaign in the current scenario," said Sakharam Bapu.

"Do we really need that much money and resources for this campaign? We can arrange many resources on our way to the north," Sadashiv Bhau who was holding his thoughts, finally spoke and questioned Raghunathrao.

"Sadashiv, you have never been on a campaign to the north. You have no idea how difficult and costly it is to run a campaign there!" Raghunath was not happy with the statement.

"There is no need to argue on this. We will think about this and decide on the campaign. Ahmad Shah is not a ruler of a small kingdom. We need the resources and the strategy to counter his moves," Nanasaheb announced and dispersed the darbar.

"Shrimant, you are aware of the financial situation. We can't afford the amount asked by Raghunathrao," said Sadashiv Bhau, who was in Nanasaheb Peshwa's chamber.

Nanasaheb got up from his seat and paced around, impatiently rubbing his right hand on his forehead. He stopped near the window and looked outside like he was trying to gauge the situation in which the empire was.

"I know, Sadashiv. But we can't deny the facts which Raghunathrao shared in the full darbar. I know what he is asking is not possible and is also not required, but we should respect his experience of campaigns in the north and should listen if he suggests something," Nanasaheb said thoughtfully.

"Shrimant, you are right, but Raghunathrao spends too much money on campaigns. He is popular in north about his ways of working and splurging money on unnecessary indulgences."

"Yes, he has some flaws, but he is still our best man to lead the Marathas in north against Ahmad Shah. I am concerned about our financial situation at this time. How we will arrange the resources for the campaign?" Nanasaheb spoke fondly about his brother.

"I agree with you Shrimant. I will sit with Bapu and check the treasury to see how much money we can allocate for this campaign."

"We do not have any other option, but to fight Ahmad Shah and protect our motherland from these barbaric invaders, Sadashiv. Ahmad Shah has got used to invading our motherland and destroying our cities for many years now. He has to be stopped, confronted, and defeated." Nanasaheb told Sadashiv Bhau. Both of them were standing near the window and were looking outside, appreciating the beauty of Poona city which had seen many destructions since the time of Shivaji.

Sadashiv Bhau talked to Nanasaheb about some potential revenue sources in the north and then left him alone in his chamber. Nanasaheb was still in deep thoughts about the situation in Delhi when Gopikabai entered the chamber.

"Are you still concerned about the campaign against Abdali?" Gopikabai asked her husband. She always kept a track of proceedings in darbar and administrative activities of the empire.

"Marathas are never scared of their enemies. We have enough warriors in our empire who can fight against him and defeat him. I am not concerned about the campaign. I am concerned about the resources," Nanasaheb responded.

"You are right. Marathas have always defeated enemies and the same would be the fate of Abdali in Delhi. Do you remember how bravely Vishwas fought in the Udgir campaign? Everyone was talking about him after the campaign. Even Sadashiv was appreciating the skills of our son." Gopikabai intentionally spoke about the bravado of their son.

The decision to lead the campaign against Ahmad Shah was still not taken. Gopikabai was aware of the experience of Raghunathrao in the north and the fondness of her husband for Sadashiv. She was jealous of these two as they had overshadowed her son.

"I am proud that Vishwas has shown his valor in the battle at Udgir. Sadashiv had told me how bravely he fought and supported him. He is the grandson of great Bajirao Peshwa and I am confident that he would carry forward the legacy of his grandfather." Nanasaheb appreciated his son. Led by Sadashiv Bhau, Marathas had won that battle a few months back.

"You are right, he will carry forward the legacy of great Bajirao Peshwa. I think now is the right time that he should get an opportunity to lead a campaign," Gopikabai expressed her feelings to her husband.

Nanasaheb was aware of the challenges of the campaign in the north and was little surprised when Gopikabai suggested their son's name. Vishwasrao was the eldest son of Nanasaheb and the natural heir to the Peshwai, but Nanasaheb thought that he was too young to lead a major campaign.

* * *

There was silence in the darbar. Sadashiv had shared the financial condition of the treasury with everyone. Nanasaheb Peshwa had got up from the musnud and paced around the darbar, impatiently rubbing his wrinkled hands on his forehead.

Nanasaheb had asked everyone to share their thoughts, but when no one spoke, he stopped next to Sadashiv Bhau.

"What options do we have Sadashiv?" Nanasaheb mumbled.

"Shrimant, all of us who are present in the darbar today know the financial situation and in such a situation, we can't afford the expense suggested by Raghunathrao. Even if we take a loan, it would be difficult to manage that debt later. We already have a large debt to repay." Sadashiv openly shared his thoughts and stared towards Raghunathrao, conveying to him that his demand could not be met.

"Battles are not fought with bare hands and empty stomachs. If we want to defeat Ahmad Shah, then we need a sizeable army and the money to keep them ready for the battle," Raghunathrao responded in a terse tone.

"I understand your point Raghunathrao and we are here to discuss the options. Sadashiv, Raghunathrao is right. If we can't afford the money, we should not plan this campaign." Nanasaheb felt dejected. Sadashiv Bhau gauged the mood of the darbar.

"Battles are not fought with money or with soldiers or with guns. Battlers are fought with willpower and resolve; battles are fought with a zeal to sacrifice yourself to protect your motherland. Money can buy you the guns, but can't guarantee victory in the battle. Shrimant, I know that we need resources to fight against Ahmad Shah, but those resources necessarily don't have to come from our treasury or the state," Sadashiv Bhau tried to lift the mood of the Peshwa and those who were present in the darbar.

"It is good to be patriotic and passionate for your motherland, but it is more important to be pragmatic. I am curious to know your plans to confront Ahmad Shah. Sadashiv, can you explain your strategy to all of us here in the darbar?" Nanasaheb was impressed by Sadashiv, who had given him some hope.

"If I were to lead this campaign, then all I need is a cavalry of ten thousand horsemen and five-thousand-foot soldiers. I would also need ten lakh rupees to manage the campaign!" Sadashiv surprised everyone with his statement. There were murmurs across the darbar; some were appreciating his thoughts while some were criticizing.

"You are not going to fight the Nizam at Udgir, Sadashiv. You are going to fight Ahmad Shah Abdali of Afghanistan," Raghunathrao said sarcastically with a cunning smile on his face. He had sensed the mood of the darbar which was in two minds after hearing Sadashiv Bhau's statement.

"We can march from Poona to the north with that size of troops. On our way, we will talk to all our allies for financial and military support to fight against Ahmad Shah. We are going to protect the whole Hindustan against invaders. Ahmad Shah is a danger to all the kingdoms in the north. I believe we can garner a large contingent and resources to fight against him!" Sadashiv was undeterred by Raghunathrao's sarcasm and explained his plan to the Peshwa.

"There is no guarantee that we will get any support in the north, marching with this size of army and resources would turn this into a suicidal mission," retorted Raghunathrao.

"Raghunathrao!" Nanasaheb tried to show his disagreement to his brother. He got up from the musnud and walked towards Raghunathrao. There was tension in the darbar.

"You are our most experienced commander in the north and I expect constructive discussion from you. I would like to hear a solution, we all know the problem and have discussed it enough." Nanasaheb told him calmly. Raghunathrao sensed that it was a signal from him to stop, so he moved back a few steps.

"Shrimant, I am speaking based on my experience only. In any battle, it is very important to know your strengths and weaknesses," Raghunathrao chose his words carefully. Nanasaheb heard his brother, nodded slowly, and then walked towards Sadashiv Bhau.

"We don't have much of a choice now; this battle has to be fought. If Sadashiv is confident that he can manage this campaign with limited resources, then he is the best-suited person for this campaign."

The announcement by Nanasaheb was surprising for everyone in the court. Sadashiv Bhau was a capable leader who had proven himself on the battlefield, but had never been to the north. The lack of experience and limited resources could prove dangerous for the battle.

Raghunathrao was astonished by the announcement. He was expecting to be declared the leader of the campaign. The rising stature of Sadashiv Bhau had already been a concern for him and the campaign against Ahmad Shah would be a major battle.

"Shrimant! Campaigns in the north are always difficult and against Ahmad Shah, the experience of the north would be a big advantage." Raghunathrao shared his thoughts.

"I know and I give charge of assisting Sadashiv on this campaign to Raghunathrao," declared Nanasaheb. Raghunathrao was agitated, he was breathing heavily and was looking at the floor with anger.

"Shrimant, please forgive my words, but I think such high dependency on allies in the north is not a good idea. I have my apprehensions about the support from allies in the north. I would like to withdraw myself from this campaign." Raghunathrao stunned everyone in the darbar and went against the decision of the Peshwa.

"Raghunathrao! This is an order," Nanasaheb said in a loud voice. Raghunathrao nodded his head in disagreement and left the darbar.

* * *

"On that day you said that Vishwas will carry forward the legacy of his grandfather, but for that he needs opportunities," Gopikabai was talking to her husband.

"Raghunathrao disobeyed my order in the darbar today." Nanasaheb was still thinking about the happenings in the darbar.

"Everything happens for good," Gopikabai said.

"There is nothing good in this. Raghunathrao is very important for this campaign and his absence could prove very costly for the empire."

"This is the right opportunity for Vishwas to prepare himself to lead the campaigns for the Maratha empire."

Nanasaheb heard the statement made by Gopikabai who was speaking out of love and with limited knowledge of the battlefield.

"Sadashiv is the most suited person to lead this campaign to the north, but he also needs Raghunathrao's support. Vishwas is too young to lead this," Nanasaheb responded.

"For a father, the children are always young. At this age, you had become Peshwa," Gopikabai said, the statement brought a smile to the face of the Peshwa, who finally gave in to his wife's demands.

"I will talk to Sadashiv about this and Vishwas can join him on this campaign." Nanasaheb told Gopikabai, who was happy that her eldest son and the heir apparent of the Maratha empirc would go on the most important campaign for Marathas.

* * *

On the 14th day of the year 1761, the third battle of Panipat was fought between Marathas and Ahmad Shah. Both the sides camped near Panipat for many months and waited for the right time. Ahmad Shah successfully managed to cut the food supplies to the Maratha contingent which had more than a lakh people in their camps comprising of soldiers, women, children, and aged people. As the supplies dwindled, it made Marathas desperate and on the morning of Makar Sankranti, Marathas led by Sadashiv Bhau went to the battlefield.

The Battle of Panipat had been a big setback for the Marathas who not only lost the battle, but also lost Sadashiv Bhau, Shamsher Bahadur, and the heir apparent Vishwasrao. Nanasaheb's health deteriorated further, and he could not bear the trauma of losing his loved ones in Panipat. A few months after the battle, Nanasaheb left for the heavenly abode. The death of Nanasaheb Peshwa sent tremors across the Maratha empire. For the first time, the empire witnessed a succession crisis for Peshwai.

Nanasaheb had three sons, the eldest one had already died in Panipat and his second son, Madhavrao, was just sixteen years old at that time. There were murmurs inside Shaniwar Wada about who would be the next Peshwa.

"Dadasaheb, this is the right time for you to take charge of the Maratha empire. You are the eldest member of the family now and have experience in leading campaigns across the continent." Sakharam Bapu was in the chamber of Raghunathrao.

"Tomorrow we all are meeting in the darbar and we will see what decision is made by all the ministers," Raghunathrao was sure that he would get the support of everyone in the darbar.

"The ministers have already made a choice and you have not been informed. You are very naïve Dadasaheb that you still trust the ministers," Sakharam Bapu said cunningly.

"Bapu, let us wait till tomorrow for the darbar to discuss the topic of succession. I trust that they don't have much of a choice," Raghunathrao spoke with a smile on his face. He was eyeing the post of Peshwa.

At that time, Raghunathrao was twenty-six-year-old and was the eldest member of the Peshwa family, who had years of experience in leading successful campaigns. His bravery was known to everyone, but his behaviour of spending too much during the campaigns and his indulgence in women was an eyesore for most of the ministers who detested him for this. Being the younger brother of Nanasaheb, Raghunathrao thought that he was a natural choice for the post of Peshwa after his brother's death. For over four decades, since the time of Balaji Vishwanath Peshwa, the Peshwai had remained in the Bhat family and had become hierarchical. Raghunathrao, being the only alive son of Bajirao Peshwa, was in line to take the charge.

The subject of succession was discussed many times in the darbar, which remained divided between the two potential claimants of the throne - Raghunathrao and Madhavrao. Raghunathrao had his group of supporters led by Sakharam Bapu and Madhavrao was supported by Trimbakrao and Ram Shastri.

When no consensus was reached, Trimbakrao approached Tarabai. Tarabai was the daughter-in-law of Shivaji and had a strong influence on the Marathas despite her old age at that time. She had expressed her views on the succession after the death of Nanasaheb and supported Madhavrao for the Peshwai.

"Last year has been very difficult for the empire. We have lost not only battles, but so many of our loved ones. Panipat has been a setback for the Marathas, but we have to move ahead. This seat of Marathas should not remain empty for too long." Trimbakrao spoke in the darbar which was deliberating on the succession.

"I told Shrimant Nanasaheb about the campaign, but at that time, no one listened to me. We wanted our army to fight without any resources and we sent an inexperienced commander to lead the campaign. This campaign was destined to fail from the beginning. Ahmad Shah did not win the battle of Panipat. It was us who lost it due to our poor planning," Raghunathrao spoke to everyone.

"Victory and loss are a part of battles. Sometimes we lose, while sometimes we win, but the efforts of those who sacrificed their lives should not be belittled." Trimbakrao was not happy with what Raghunathrao had said.

"There is no point in talking about what has already happened. Let us discuss the future of the empire..." Sakharam Bapu tried to diffuse the tension. "We have had multiple discussions among all the ministers and considered the opinion of Maharani Tarabai. After many deliberations, all the ministers concluded that Madhavrao Bhat would be the next Peshwa of the Maratha empire and Raghunathrao Bhat would be his regent," Trimbakrao declared in the court.

The decision received a mixed response from the darbar; there were murmurs across. Raghunathrao got up from his seat, he wanted to say something, but controlled his anger and left the darbar in haste.

In his chamber, Raghunathrao threw his sword on the floor. Anandibai, hearing the sound, rushed to the chamber where she saw her husband burning with rage.

"The bravest Maratha has been given the charge of the regent Dadasaheb," Sakharam Bapu said sarcastically. Anandibai looked at her husband with sympathy. '*He deserved the Peshwai,*' she thought.

"You were right, Bapu. I no longer trust the Maratha ministers," Raghunathrao said. There was pain and anger in his voice.

"You have to fight your own battle, Swari," said Anandibai.

Raghunathrao looked towards her, trying to decipher what she had just said. He was exhausted, so he threw his *pagdi* on the floor, and fell on his bed.

Raghunathrao's dream of becoming Peshwa had been shattered.

A REBEL IN THE FAMILY

Madhavrao Peshwa was present in the darbar with his ministers and they were deliberating on the counter against the offensives of Nizam Ali who had become a big threat to the Marathas. Sakharam Bapu, Nana Phadnis, Raghunathrao and other dignitaries were present and were engaged in the discussion. It was a tense moment in the darbar as ministers were still uncomfortable with a young Peshwa at the helm. On top of it, they also had to deal with the irrational behaviour of Raghunathrao.

"We have to send a strong message to Nizam Ali and there is only one way to do that. We have to attack forts in his territory." Madhavrao told the darbar, but the suggestion was not liked by many.

Only a few months had passed since Madhavrao had taken charge of the empire. He had faced constant interference in most of his decisions either by his uncle or his mother. Both not only undermined the position of the Peshwa, but also expressed their keenness to keep control over the activities of the empire.

Nizam Ali had been a trouble for the Marathas for a long time now. Not only had he learned about the differences between Raghunathrao and Madhavrao, but was also aware of the financial condition of the Marathas. He was preparing his army to charge into the Maratha territory. The family dispute and an inexperienced leader at the helm of the affairs had only motivated him further.

"We have exhausted all our resources in Panipat, Madhav. We don't have any funds left to fight any battle, forget about fighting a powerful Nizam!" Raghunathrao confronted the Peshwa.

Madhavrao was young and had limited administrative experience, but he was a very composed person with strong control on his emotions. The last few months had been difficult for him , but he remained calm in the darbar.

Madhavrao got up from his seat, walked around the darbar for a few moments, and then stood in front of his uncle.

"What has happened can't be changed, Kaka. It fills my heart with pain when I think about Panipat, but that doesn't mean we should stop fighting for the empire. In fact, we should fight with more determination. Perhaps one day we will be able to avenge the loss of Panipat also!" Madhavrao spoke with passion to his uncle and ministers.

Raghunathrao smirked listening to the immature response from his nephew. He would not let him go so easily.

"I had requested Nanasaheb to allow me to lead the Maratha army at Panipat, but he did not listen to me. The loss at Panipat has been such a disgrace to the Marathas. All our enemies are laughing at us and looking for opportunities to attack. We have lost so many allies in the north. Sooner or later, it was bound to happen..." Raghunathrao again initiated the discussion on Panipat. Madhavrao was getting agitated, but out of respect for his uncle, he tried to dissuade the situation.

"Kaka, we can't change what has happened in the past. It would be good if we discuss our plans." Madhavrao tried to change the direction of the discussion.

"Battles are fought with money and resources Madhav; you are too young to understand this and..." Raghunathrao was stopped in the middle of his sentence by the Peshwa.

"Battles are fought and won by willpower, Kaka. Money is just a medium. No army can win a battle just by having money. You need soldiers who are willing to sacrifice their lives for their soil. You need leaders who can die for the sake of their motherland." Madhavrao said authoritatively and conveyed his discomfort to his uncle, but Raghunathrao was not one to give in so easily.

"I believe you, Madhav. You can gather any army with your inspirational words," Raghunathrao mocked his nephew and left the darbar. Madhavrao remained seated, and took a deep breath. He wanted to order his uncle to stop, but decided against it. The ministers present in the darbar were silently observing them.

"Shrimant, forgive me for saying this in darbar, but Dadasaheb is right. We need funds to fight Nizam. You are already aware of the financial situation. We have huge debts after the loss at Panipat," Sakharam Bapu supported the stand of Raghunathrao.

"I understand that, Bapu. We should find a way to get funds and plan the campaign. I am not convinced that the absence of funds means we should not protect ourselves."

It was becoming difficult for Madhavrao to hold onto the affairs of the state with constant differences with his uncle and continuous interference of his mother. Later in the day, he was in his mother's chamber to discuss the issue of Nizam and the situation of the treasury.

"I have invited Kaka also, but I am not sure if he will come," Madhavrao told Gopikabai.

"You were right in darbar today, Madhav; it is the time to stop Nizam before he does further damage. I think it would be good if your Kaka leads this campaign against Nizam," Gopikabai told his son. Madhavrao looked a bit puzzled by the suggestion.

"Kaka has his way of working. He doesn't listen to us in the darbar. Even now, when I invited him to come to meet you here, he has disregarded that request by not being here. I am worried how much he would listen to us on the battlefield." Madhavrao was not happy with the advice given by his mother.

"I know how your Kaka works. That is the reason I want him to lead this campaign."

"As you say, aaosaheb," Madhavrao folded his hands in respect and bowed in front of his mother to leave. He was not comfortable with the suggestion given by her. At that time Marathas could not have afforded a loss in the battle and giving charge to Raghunathrao would surely mean a loss.

Gopikabai had underestimated the capabilities of his son and was protecting him against the imminent danger in the battle. Nizam Ali had a strong army and Gopikabai thought that it would be better if Raghunathrao would lead the campaign. If the campaign was successful, Madhavrao would get the credit and if it failed, Raghunathrao would get the blame. She was safeguarding the reputation of her son who had just taken the charge of Peshwai.

Nizam Ali was marching towards Poona. On his way, he was destroying many religious places of Hindus. Scindia's fort at Shrigonda had also faced the brunt of his anger. Nizam Ali was closing on Poona and Madhavrao had understood his intentions.

"There are two ways to counter Nizam. One is to attack Aurangabad. That would send a message to Nizam. The second way is a diplomatic one. We talk to our sympathizers in his camp," said Madhavrao. He was sitting in his chamber with Gopikabai, Sakharam Bapu and Raghunathrao to plan the strategy against Nizam.

"Can we take the risk of leaving Poona at this time? What if Nizam Ali plans an attack on Poona?" Raghunathrao questioned the first option.

"Attacking his territory will send a strong message to Nizam Ali and he will think twice in the future to march towards Poona. This comes with a risk that he might come and attack us in Poona." Madhavrao assessed the situation and the group further deliberated on the strategy.

It was decided that first they would take the diplomatic route and Trimbakrao was assigned the task of initiating talks with Ramchandra Jadhav and Mir Mughal. The diplomatic approach was taken to avoid a war and unnecessarily burden the empire with more debts.

In the days to come, Trimbakrao was successful in initiating the discussions with sympathizers in the camp of Nizam Ali.

"Ram Chandra has agreed to support us and he said that Mir Mughal is also ready to join our camp. We must agree to their terms," Trimbakrao said. Madhavrao was in his chamber along with his ministers.

"You can discuss and negotiate with Ram Chandra on my behalf, Mama." Madhavrao gave full powers to Trimbakrao to finalize the terms of the agreement.

"There had been skirmishes with the Nizam's army near Chas for the last two days. We have been successful in keeping them at bay from Poona," Trimbakrao shared more updates. When the diplomatic channels were initiated, Trimbakrao kept some troops ready and confronted the Nizam to avoid any suspicion.

Nizam Ali had suffered some losses. Through his strategy and diplomatic outreach, Madhavrao had finally convinced Ramchandra Jadhav and Mir Mughal, Nizam Ali's brother, to join Marathas and fight against Nizam Ali. As the diplomatic outreach was successful and Nizam Ali's army stood divided, it was time to send a signal for war. A force of around seventy thousand was ready to fight Nizam Ali who was camping at Chas, just a day-march away from Poona.

Marathas had the upper hand at that time as Nizam had walked into their stronghold. As expected, within a few days, Nizam sent a message to the Peshwa for a treaty.

"Nizam wants to sign a peace treaty. Considering our current situation, it would be good for us to sign a treaty with him. I will go with my contingent to sign a treaty with Nizam," Raghunathrao said enthusiastically in darbar.

"I agree with you, Kaka. It is not the time for further confrontation. A treaty with Nizam would be a better option. Tomorrow we would decide who would go to Nizam to negotiate the terms of the peace treaty." Madhavrao was apprehensive about the intentions of his uncle. He was aware of the cordial relationship his uncle once had with Nizam.

The decision did not go well with Raghunathrao, who had hidden intentions of strengthening his relations with Nizam through this treaty. To undermine the position of Peshwa, Raghunathrao decided to involve Gopikabai in the discussion.

"Come, Madhav..." Gopikabai welcomed Madhavrao into her chamber. Raghunathrao was already there.

"Your Kaka wants to lead the negotiations with Nizam."

"I know, he told me that in darbar today. I have not made any decision in this regard, but his suggestion would be given due consideration," Madhavrao said authoritatively.

"Vahinisaheb, I would take your leave now," Raghunathrao said. He had no intentions to convince his nephew. He had already shared his mind with Gopikabai.

"Do you want to send someone else to negotiate the terms of this treaty?" asked Gopikabai once Raghunathrao left.

"I want to send Trimbakrao Mama for the negotiations. We all are aware of Kaka's closeness with Nizam."

"I know, Madhav. But if we are not able to get favourable terms in the treaty, it might harm your image and your future as a leader," his mother said.

Gopikabai had closely observed the activities of the empire during the rule of her husband. She had shared her opinion many times with Nanasaheb also. It was she who had suggested sending Vishwasrao to Panipat. Her political knowledge was respected by many in the empire. Madhavrao had just taken the charge and Nizam was a strong enemy. Her perspective was very simple. Any unfavourable terms in the treaty would only undermine the position of her son and give an upper hand to Raghunathrao.

Madhavrao decided not to escalate the matter further and agreed to the suggestion of his mother. Raghunathrao went to negotiate with Nizam Ali and a treaty was signed. Marathas surrendered territory worth forty lacs of revenue. The treaty was resented by many ministers in the darbar and Raghunathrao was accused of harbouring soft feelings for Nizam Ali.

The incident had its impact on Madhavrao, who became more assertive and slowly took full control of state affairs. Raghunathrao felt threatened by his nephew and dramatically suggested retiring from all the affairs of the empire, which was accepted by the Peshwa. Trimbakrao was appointed as Karbhari along with Baburao Phadnis. Sakharam Bapu, a close aid of Raghunathrao and a senior minister in the empire was also removed from his post. Raghunathrao had no intentions of retiring; it was just deception. As a result, he had lost control of the administrative activities of the empire. The removal of Sakharam Bapu as Karbhari was a big setback for Raghunathrao, whose influence on state affairs was slowly fading away.

"Dadasaheb, I have no intentions to continue working in Shaniwar Wada now. Shrimant has released me from all the duties and I would be staying at my Wada, away from all the worldly desires and administrative activities." Sakharam Bapu was with Raghunathrao in his chamber.

"I can understand your feelings Bapu, what happened is not right. I promise you that we would soon get a deserving place in Shaniwar Wada," Raghunathrao replied.

"I don't see any future for myself at Shaniwar Wada. I am worried about your future, Dadasaheb."

"Nizam Ali is on our side and has promised financial and military support," Raghunathrao told Sakharam Bapu. Sakharam was an experienced politician and he had inklings of the intentions of Nizam Ali.

Those were not the times to trust a Mughal, and astute politician Sakharam Bapu was aware of that.

* * *

"Shastribuwa, What other option do we have with us? This can't go forever with Kaka. I have given him so many chances. We all had discussed this with him, but he is not willing to cooperate. He wants to rule," Madhavrao and Ram Shastri were in the camp near Alegaon. Raghunathrao had sided with Nizam Ali and had challenged the Peshwa on the battlefield.

"Shrimant, Dadasaheb is a good warrior, but do you think he would be a good ruler for Marathas?" Ram Shastri fearlessly questioned Madhavrao.

"This family dispute is not good for the empire, Shastribuwa. If the only solution for this is that Kaka takes charge of the empire, I would happily hand over Peshwai to him and retire," Madhavrao was in a pensive mood.

The Maratha army had faced a difficult day in the battle at Alegaon with several casualties. It was a matter of a few days before they lost the battle to the forces led by Raghunathrao who had the support of Nizam Ali. Raghunathrao had revolted openly and despite many rounds of negotiations, had not agreed to any treaty with the Peshwa.

Raghunathrao had cleared his intentions. He wanted the throne, and he was ready to fight a war against his people for the Peshwai.

"Shrimant, if you allow, we can send Nana to negotiate on your behalf," Ram Shastri suggested.

"This is a family matter, Shastribuwa. No one would go to negotiate with Kaka on my behalf. As the leader of the Marathas, it is my responsibility to resolve this."

More than a year had passed since Madhavrao took charge of Peshwai, but despite all his efforts, he could not convince his uncle to support him. Standing in the camp on that day with his ministers around him, Madhavrao felt dejected and had given up on his uncle.

All the ministers and generals were stunned when they saw the Peshwa dressed in his full attire and calling for his horse.

"Shrimant?" Malharrao Holkar came rushing to him.

"I am going to Kaka's camp to surrender and accept all his terms," Madhavrao said in a somber voice. Though the generals were aware of the situation on the battlefield, no one expected that Madhavrao would surrender so easily.

"I will join you, Shrimant," requested Malharrao who was a senior and reputed Maratha general from Indore.

"No one will come with me. You can follow me from a distance," Madhavrao said firmly and rode his horse towards Raghunathrao's camp.

Madhavrao was pained by the actions of his uncle, who had created a tricky situation for the Peshwa. At a time when he should be fighting his enemies, he had to fight his uncle. All the allies were looking at him with hope. It was the most testing moment for Madhavrao; he knew he could not win his uncle with force.

This was the moment that would define the future of Madhavrao Peshwa.

The sky was slowly changing its colour from bright orange to pale yellow as the sun was about to set and birds were returning to their nests. Madhavrao Peshwa was on his horse, riding towards the enemy camp, alone.

When soldiers in Raghunathrao's camp saw the dust rising from the direction of the enemy's camp, they rushed to inform him and he immediately came out to check. Moments later, they could see someone riding on a horse coming towards them. As the rider came closer, it became clear who it was. As Madhavrao stopped near Raghunathrao's tent and dismounted, he was immediately surrounded by soldiers.

"Kaka, I have come to talk to you in private," Madhavrao said calmly. There were no emotions on his face. Raghunathrao ordered his guards to keep a watch for any unwanted activities.

"Madhav, I told you that you are too young to manage the affairs of the state, but you did not listen to me," Raghunathrao said with a cunning smile on his face. He sensed that he had finally defeated his nephew.

"Kaka, I don't want to fight a battle with you. We are family and if we will fight with each other, what message would we send to our allies and our enemies?" Madhavrao openly expressed his feelings to his uncle.

"If you care so much for the family, then you should have known who deserves to be the Peshwa," Raghunathrao said angrily and sat on his seat. Madhavrao was still standing in front of his uncle.

It became clear to Madhavrao that his uncle won't give up on his wish to be Peshwa. He went close to his uncle and put his hands on his pagdi. Madhavrao contemplated his decision and then took off his pagdi and kept it on the table on his right. Madhavrao sat on the ground in front of Raghunathrao who was proudly sitting on the seat. Raghunathrao was feeling smug. He had defeated the Peshwa who was sitting helplessly in front of him on the ground and was at his mercy.

"You are like a father figure to me. I request you not to insult this great seat of Marathas just for the sake of power. I am ready to hand over the Peshwai to you and retire to Banaras," Madhavrao stood and went closer to Raghunathrao.

"Don't disgrace the family, Kaka. I beg you not to do this and set a wrong precedence. I have kept my pagdi next to you on the table out of respect. I could not keep it at your feet as it would be disrespect to the Peshwai, else I would have done that. I hand over the Peshwai to you at this very moment." Madhavrao bent in front of Raghunathrao, put his head on the feet of his uncle, and surrendered the Peshwai.

Raghunathrao was stunned by the gesture of the Peshwa, who after all was his nephew and like his son. It was an emotional scene inside the tent. Raghunathrao did not move for a while, unable to react in that situation. The pagdi of the Peshwa was lying on the table next to him and he had been handed over the Peshwai.

Raghunathrao looked at the pagdi and then at his nephew who was still bent in front of him. He slowly put his hands on the shoulders of Madhavrao, hinting him to get up.

"Kaka, you take the Peshwai and I will retire from all the affairs of the empire and go to Kashi."

With tears of Madhavrao touching his feet, Raghunathrao was overcome by emotions and could not control himself. His eyes were filled with tears of guilt. He helped Madhavrao to get up and hugged him.

"Madhav, you are like my son. I have no intentions of becoming Peshwa. It should be me who should retire to Kashi, not you." Raghunathrao took the pagdi of Peshwa in his hands and kept it back on Madhavrao's head.

"Whatever you want, Kaka. I will agree to everything," Madhavrao said.

Raghunathrao did not accept the Peshwai, but he managed to assert his control over Madhavrao. Sakharam Bapu was reinstated as the Karbhari and Trimbakrao and Baburao Phadnis were removed from their posts. Raghunathrao agreed to give back the territory worth sixty lacs of revenue which was surrendered by Nizam at Udgir. Nizam also got the fort of Daulatabad. Furthermore, Raghunathrao tried to put restrictions on Madhavrao's movement.

Raghunathrao returned the favour of Nizam Ali for his support, but his friendship with Nizam Ali proved costly for Poona.

Nizam wanted to extract more from Marathas and again planned a campaign to Poona.

"Nizam has sent his demands, Shrimant." Sakharam Bapu read the demands in the court.

It was a tense atmosphere in the darbar. Nizam had sent his unreasonable demands to Madhavrao. If accepted, it would put the independence of the Maratha empire at stake. Madhavrao did not respond. First, he wanted to listen to Raghunathrao.

"We have to take action, Shrimant." Sakharam Bapu suggested.

"You are the senior-most minister Bapu and an experienced politician; you suggest what we should do in such a scenario?" Madhavrao asked Sakharam Bapu.

"We have to counter Nizam Ali. There is no other way, Madhav," Raghunathrao finally spoke.

Madhavrao had learned his lessons at the battle of Alegaon and he had keenly observed all the activities of Raghunathrao and his supporters in the empire. Peshwa, who was under pressure and consistently undermined by his uncle, was waiting for one moment to strike.

This was that moment for Madhavrao Peshwa.

An army of around fifty thousand soldiers was gathered and under the command of Madhavrao, they decided to attack Aurangabad and plundered the city. Janoji Bhosle had joined hands with Nizam and was destroying Maratha territory along the river Bhima. The Peshwa army marched towards Nagpur to teach a lesson to Janoji Bhosle and plundered the city. The hostilities between the Peshwa and Nizam continued for a few months.

Nizam was getting impatient as he was not able to defeat Marathas; who surprised him and avoided a direct battle with his forces. It was difficult for Nizam to move from one place to the other with his heavy artillery. Frustrated with months of skirmishes, Nizam Ali decided to hit the Marathas where it would hurt the most.

Poona had a terrible fate. Nizam Ali attacked the city which was caught unaware as Madhavrao and Raghunathrao both were on their respective campaigns. Many temples were destroyed, houses were burnt down and people ran for their lives. When the news reached Madhavrao, he immediately started marching towards Poona. To avoid a direct war, Nizam Ali decided to leave the Maratha capital and rushed towards Aurangabad.

As monsoon was approaching, Nizam had planned to cross the Ghod river to reach Aurangabad. He wanted to avoid any further conflict with Marathas as his position had weakened after some of his allies defected. In the middle of the night, he crossed the river and left Vitthal Sunder as the in-charge of the troops. Nizam with his troops managed to cross, but due to heavy artillery from the army, Vitthal Sunder could not cross the river with Nizam. The position of the Nizam's army was further weakened as now it stood divided into two parts.

When Madhavrao learned about the planned escape of Nizam's army to Aurangabad, he decided to attack immediately. The sudden attack by the Peshwa army surprised Vitthal Sunder, but he was prepared to face them, even with a smaller contingent.

Vitthal Sunder and his army put a strong resistance to the army of Peshwa. Marathas were getting the upper hand in the battle when suddenly Raghunathrao, who had marched straight into the enemy's forward formation, was surrounded by Vitthal Sunder and his troops. Vitthal Sunder brutally killed the troops of Raghunathrao and he was left with very few soldiers around him. Vitthal Sunder sensed the opportunity of finishing the leader of the enemy and immediately charged at Raghunathrao.

Madhavrao, who was fighting some distance away, saw that his uncle had been surrounded by Vitthal Sunder and was in danger. Madhavrao directed his troops towards Raghunathrao and led the charge. Madhavrao jumped from his elephant and fought with ferocity to save his uncle and overpowered Nizam's army. Vitthal Sunder was killed within sometime and Nizam's army was decimated.

The Treaty of Aurangabad was signed post the battle and the Marathas got eighty lacs worth of territories. The battle was the first major victory of Madhavrao Peshwa who rose to prominence in later years and became an undisputed leader of the Maratha empire.

A TRAGIC END 4

November 1772
Chintamani Temple, Theur

The sun had already set and slowly the darkness had engulfed the area. One could hear the sound of the water from the river. The water which was flowing down the stream, cutting the soil at the shore on its way. There were camps of Maratha troops and chiefs near the river and around the Chintamani temple. It had become a base of Madhavrao Peshwa for over a month.

Narayanrao was sitting on the bank of the river, alone. Two guards were standing at a distance from him. He was looking at the water flowing down the stream. Narayanrao had faint memories of the Panipat battle, but he learned about the loss later from his mother, Parvatibai, and other family members. The Peshwa family had suffered the biggest blow in that battle. A long time had passed since that debacle, but the Bhat family had not forgotten the loss.

Narayanrao was thinking about the events of earlier in the day when his brother was in the court and was coughing constantly. At one point, he had even coughed blood. After the loss of his father and eldest brother, Narayanrao had developed a strong bond of love and respect for Madhavrao. It pained him to see his brother in such a state.

One thing my brother could not beat is this disease, thought Narayanrao. He got up and with heavy feet, started walking towards the Chintamani temple where his brother was praying to Lord Ganesha.

It was time for the evening aarti at the temple. The flag on the temple was flying high. Narayanrao could hear the ringing of the bells and chants of the evening aarti.

'*Lord Ganesha, please do some miracle,*' Narayanrao folded his hands in the direction of the temple, wiped his teary eyes, and walked towards the temple. His guards followed him.

Theur represented an army camp with many Maratha chiefs arriving to meet the ailing Peshwa and pay their homage. The news of Peshwa's illness had spread far and wide. It had sent a shock wave across the royals and the common public.

Madhavrao was performing his duties from Theur. The ministers either camped there or visited Theur frequently. A palanquin had just arrived and stopped in front of the royal mansion. Ram Shastri got down from the palanquin and rushed to the chamber of Madhavrao Peshwa.

"Why have you sent an urgent message, Nana?" asked a worried Ram Shastri when he saw Nana Phadnis waiting for him in the mansion.

"Shastribuwa, Shrimant has decided to release Dadasaheb from the house arrest. You very well know the situation at Shaniwar Wada and it is only you who can convince Shrimant against this decision. Dadasaheb would not sit idle. He remembers what had happened post-Panipat. He would take this as his last chance to take the Peshwai," Nana said in a concerned voice.

"Shrimant would be having his own reasons to release Dadasaheb. It would be good if we speak to him before making any assumptions. We should go and talk to him," replied Ram Shastri.

Madhavrao Peshwa had just woken up and a servant helped him to sit with the support of a bolster. The rugged body of Peshwa looked like a skeleton. The disease had made him so weak that he could not sit and walk on his own.

Ram Shastri entered the chamber with Nana Phadnis and both saluted the Peshwa. Madhavrao had a smile on his face when he saw Ram Shastri.

"Shrimant, how is your health now?"Ram Shastri enquired.

"Vaidyaraj had told me that I will be free of all this pain very soon," Madhavrao said in a soft voice.

"Don't lose hope, Shrimant," Ram Shastri responded.

"Shastribuwa, what brings you to Theur today?" Madhavrao changed the topic. He didn't want to talk about his health.

"I heard about your health Shrimant, and came to meet you."

"There is nothing new about my health, Shastribuwa. This pain will stay with me till my last breath."

"Shrimant!" Ram Shastri was about to say something, but stopped in the middle of his sentence as Madhavrao coughed violently for a while.

A servant helped him and cleaned his face. Ram Shastri was pained to see the Peshwa who had expanded the Maratha empire from south to north in his heydays was now just a pale shadow of himself. The servant again helped Madhavrao to balance himself and sit straight against the bolster.

"Speak freely, Shastribuwa. My body might be weak, but my mind and my heart are still strong," Madhavrao said nonchalantly.

Ram Shastri looked into his eyes and saw the same spark that he had seen long ago in the eyes of the seventeen-year-old young and brave boy, who had taken the charge of Peshwai in difficult times.

“Shrimant, I have learned that you have decided to release Dadasaheb from the house arrest.”

“Shastribuwa, as the Peshwa, I fought many battles during these years. I am ready to fight many more battles if the almighty would allow me. However, this is one battle I don’t want to continue fighting,” Madhavrao said seriously.

“I understand, Shrimant, but is this the right time?”Ram Shastri questioned Madhavrao’s decision.

“There is never a right time to fight against your family members, Shastribuwa. It is not only this disease that is killing me. The behaviour of Kaka is equally hurting for me.”

“If Dadasaheb is freed at such a time, it will only lead to more chaos. I don’t see any good coming out of it for the empire,” Ram Shastri debated.

“This time I have not decided for the benefit of the empire, Shastribuwa. This decision is for the benefit of the family. This one decision is personal for me. I want to set Kaka free, so that I can die in peace, without any regrets. You can blame me for being selfish here, Shastribuwa.”

“I respect your affection for Dadasaheb. I just wish he too would reciprocate the same feeling for you when he visits you this time,” said Ram Shastri.

“Nana, send a message to Kaka and invite him to Theur. I want to discuss some important matters with him before I make any announcement,” ordered Madhavrao. The Peshwa might have lost the physical strength he once had, but his vision for Marathas was still intact. His decision to invite Raghunathrao to Theur was a part of his long-term vision for the empire.

"Sure, Shrimant," said Nana.

The empire was expecting the succession announcement from the ailing Peshwa. Nana had also sensed what Madhavrao had on his mind, but it was surprising for Nana that Madhavrao had not consulted any of his senior ministers.

'Peshwa had all the powers to make the succession decision on his own,' thought Nana.

* * *

The sound of bells coming from the Chintamani temple was making the morning blissful. Ramabai was standing near the window and was looking at the garden outside, which looked serene with Jasmine flowers. Even from a distance, she could smell the rich fragrance of the flowers. Theur was buzzing with a lot of activity and she could see the consistent movement of people, palanquins, and horses around the place even at the early morning hours. Madhavrao and Ramabai had visited Theur many times and it was on her suggestion that Jasmine had been planted some time back on the empty land near the mansion.

'Theur is such a beautiful place,' she thought, but she could no longer enjoy the beauty of anything. The last few months had been an ordeal for her. The royal physician had already given the verdict on her husband. It was she who had to decide for herself.

"Rama," Madhavrao had just woken up and called her. She slowly walked towards the bed and sat near him.

"Such a beautiful day," said Madhavrao.

"There is no beauty left for me in this world." Ramabai was crying.

"Rama, don't lose hope. Trust Lord Ganesha."

"What has Lord Ganesha done for us? I have stopped believing in god now. If there would have been a God, he would have helped us," Ramabai was in somber mood. Madhavrao tried to sit straight, but he could not. Ramabai helped him. With her support, he balanced himself and looked at her.

"You are feeling alone here in Theur and I think Parvati Kaki would be feeling alone in Poona. Why don't you call her? Her presence here will make you feel better."

"Nothing will make me feel better, but I will call *Sasubai.* She would be happy to come here and meet you," said Ramabai.

They were talking when the guard announced the arrival of Narayanrao. Ramabai went to the entrance to welcome him.

"Come Narayan..." Madhavrao welcomed his brother in his chamber.

"Dada, how are you feeling now?" asked Narayanrao.

"It is a wonderful day today," replied Madhavrao.

"You wanted to see me, Dada?" Narayanrao asked again.

"Yes, Narayan. Please come and sit with me," said Madhavrao and looked at his brother with affection. Narayanrao sat next to him. There was silence in the chamber for a while, as Madhavrao was contemplating his words.

"When I became Peshwa, I was of your age, Narayan. I had my doubts about managing state affairs at such an early age. I was not expecting that I would become Peshwa as there was Vishwas Dada, but I had to take the charge. I tried my best to manage the empire and expanded it. Only future generations will tell whether I have been successful or not," Madhavrao said with teary eyes.

"You did good, Dada. The whole empire has been in awe of your work for the last eleven years," Narayanrao said with respect for his brother.

"Thanks for your kind words, Narayan. There had been many obstacles on my path. One which I feel I could not do much about is this dispute in the family."

"Kaka is jealous of your success," said Narayanrao with anger, he understood what his brother was hinting at.

"It is beyond jealousy, Narayan. I want to tell you one thing, Kaka may or may not like me, but that does not change the fact that he is my Kaka. I give you this one piece of advice, that never try to hurt him intentionally or unintentionally."

"Sure, Dada." Narayanrao was keenly listening to his brother.

"I have invited Kaka to Theur. I want you to remain present when we talk to him tomorrow." Madhavrao told his brother and the two of them talked about their childhood memories for a long before Narayanrao left the chamber.

Madhavrao had similar feelings about Raghunathrao as many other ministers had for years - Raghunathrao was not the right person to lead the Maratha empire. He unwillingly tried to hand over the Peshwai to Raghunathrao on various occasions, but that was more to placate him. He knew that Raghunathrao lacked the qualities which were needed to be a good leader. Raghunathrao had all the capabilities to lead a campaign, but not the empire.

The worrisome part for Madhavrao was that Raghunathrao was capable enough to revolt. He had done that in the past and could do that in the future. Madhavrao wanted to take no chances and that was the reason he wanted to talk to Raghunathrao before making any announcements in presence of his senior ministers and Chief justice of the Marathas.

Even in his last days, Madhavrao was worried about the future of the Maratha empire and his younger brother.

* * *

It was a bright day in Poona and the morning was hotter than expected in November. Anandibai was elated when she heard that Madhavrao had ordered the release of her husband from house arrest.

"When are you planning to go to Theur?" Anandibai asked Raghunathrao, who had just finished his religious rituals for the day.

"I am thinking of going tomorrow. I want to go and see Madhav at the earliest," Raghunathrao replied.

"The royal physician has already given the verdict. Madhav will live for a few more days." Anandibai told Raghunathrao and waited for a response.

"I feel sad for Madhav, he is so young," replied Raghunathrao.

"I understand your concern, but what about the future of the empire after Madhav?" Anandibai continued the discussion.

"I am not worried about the empire at this time. I must go and meet Madhav."

"Swari, you are so naïve in your relationships. You have fought so many battles for the empire, defeated so many enemies, but what have you got in the end? You were made regent for Madhav, who was made Peshwa even though he had neither experience nor age at his side," Anandibai tried to play with her husband's emotions.

"I don't think this is the right time to discuss political matters."

"I think this is just the right time to discuss politics and the Peshwai. Why do you think Madhav has called you to Theur?"

"He wants to meet me and discuss some important state affairs."

"Yes. The most important state affair right now is the future of Peshwai. I am sure Madhav has already made up his mind. You have no inkling, but things are changing very fast. I feel that the power is shifting again and like earlier, you will be ignored."

"What do you mean by I will be ignored?" Raghunathrao sensed where the discussion was heading.

"Narayan is already in Theur. Ram Shastri, Nana, and Haripant are also there. I have learned that Trimbakrao would also be there tomorrow. You are being called there just to complete the formality. Madhav wants your presence when he hands over the reign of the empire. He wants your commitment and loyalty to the seat of Marathas in presence of all senior ministers," said Anandibai.

"I am not going to accept whatever Madhav would say. The decision of succession would be taken after deliberations in the darbar with senior ministers and family members. Madhav can't take that decision alone."

"Don't repeat the mistake of the past. This is the right time when you, not Madhav, decide who would be the next Peshwa. You know it very well that it can't be done without holding your sword in your hand," Anandibai told him and left him alone.

Raghunathrao remained in his chamber, contemplating his next move. His release from captivity was a big relief for him, but the sudden message from Madhavrao inviting him to Theur was intriguing. Now he understood the reason for the invite. When Nanasaheb died, he should have been made Peshwa, but to his shock, a young and inexperienced Madhavrao was declared the Peshwa.

'Would something similar happen this time too?' thought Raghunathrao.

* * *

Madhavrao was furious when he saw Raghunathrao, who had just entered the temple premises, with a sword in his hand. Peshwa had no energy to control a sword or his tears. He stared at his uncle and then closed his eyes; the pain was unbearable for him. Madhavrao controlled his emotions as he wanted to resolve the family dispute.

"Kaka, you have come to meet me like this? We are inside the temple of Gajanan and instead of flowers in your hands as offerings to Gajanan, you are holding a sword," Madhavrao spoke politely to his uncle.

"You have not invited me to offer flowers to Gajanan, Madhav. I have not come here for that either. You are paying for your karmas," Raghunathrao said sarcastically.

"My karmas, Kaka? What wrong have I done for this punishment?" Madhavrao asked philosophically.

"Your time is up Madhav; this temple is surrounded by Gardis. Without my consent, you can't make any decision about the empire," Raghunathrao declared authoritatively.

"Have you come to meet your dying nephew here, Kaka? Or have you come here to grab the power from your dying nephew?" Madhavrao was pained to hear Raghunathrao's words. His eyes were burning with rage. His Kaka had failed him every time he had tried to settle the differences. Madhavrao tried to get up, but could not manage and a servant helped him sit again.

"I have come here to claim what I deserve," Raghunathrao announced in a loud voice that echoed in the temple.

"Dadasaheb, do you think it is the right time to discuss all this? Shrimant is ill and instead of asking about his health, you are conspiring to dethrone him," Ram Shastri challenged Raghunathrao.

"Shastribuwa, things are changing in the empire. I think we should talk about the future."

"Kaka, if you think that I am too weak to defend myself and this empire, then you are wrong. I may not have the physical strength to fight a battle, but I have enough mental strength to sense a coup and stop it," Madhavrao said seriously and he again tried to get up. This time, Madhavrao managed to stand in front of his uncle, his head held high. Even in his last moments, the Peshwa was standing for his empire.

"You can't stop it now, Madhav," Raghunathrao said.

"Two things that have bothered me more than anything else in the last few months, Kaka, are this disease and you. I released you from captivity so that you would come and meet me, your nephew. But you come with your army to fight the dying Peshwa and claim the throne. You think that this Madhavrao has become so weak that you can snatch the power from him. You are wrong, Kaka. Power in Maratha empire is earned, not snatched," Madhavrao's voice echoed in the temple.

"This place is surrounded by a group of my Gardis! You can't do anything now Madhav," replied Raghunathrao.

"Nana..." Madhavrao looked towards Nana Phadnis.

"Shrimant, all the Gardis have been captured," Nana responded.

"Nana, if any of the Gardis try to do anything mischievous, sever their heads from their bodies without giving it a second thought." Madhavrao thundered. Raghunathrao was shocked to learn what had just happened.

"What happened to my Gardis?" Raghunathrao looked towards Nana Phadnis.

"Kaka, let us discuss the important matters for which I had called you here," Madhavrao said calmly as the enemy had been defeated.

Nana Phadnis had learned about Raghunathrao's plan to revolt and had deployed large troops, led by Haripant Phadke, in Theur to tackle any unwanted situation. When Nana saw a large group of Gardis coming to Theur with Raghunathrao, he planned to surround and capture all of them at the opportune moment. Oblivious to all this, Raghunathrao entered the Chintamani temple to claim the throne from Madhavrao.

"Nana, can you call Narayan?" Madhavrao asked.

Narayanrao entered the temple with Nana and sat close to Madhavrao. Ram Shastri, Sakharam Bapu, and Ichchharam Pant had also arrived at the temple.

"As all of you know that I don't have much time left with me. Doctors have already given up. I have fought and won many battles for the empire. With your support and with many Maratha allies, I have expanded the empire. I have no regrets in my heart, I have received love and respect from so many people that I could never repay. I have one dying request to you, Kaka,"

Madhavrao looked towards Raghunathrao. There were tears in his eyes. Raghunathrao stood up from his place and went closer to Madhavrao. He tenderly held his hand.

"Madhav, tell me Madhav..." Raghunathrao replied emotionally. His demeanour had changed.

"You are the eldest member of the family, Kaka. Promise me that you will protect Narayan as your son." Madhavrao requested with folded hands.

"Madhav, Narayan is mine. He is my son and till I am alive, nothing will happen to him. I promise you this in front of Gajanan," Raghunathrao made the promise.

"Thank you, Kaka. It has relieved me of a big burden. Now I can die in peace," said Madhavrao. The cough was back and he had to wait for a few moments before he spoke again.

"I have one more announcement to make. Today, in front of Gajanan and in your presence, I declare Narayanrao Bhat as the next Peshwa of Marathas and Kaka as his regent.

* * *

"Shastribuwa, Kaka's behaviour is still of concern to me. Narayan is short-tempered and Kaka, even at this age, is immature. I am worried for Narayan," Madhavrao was in his chamber with Ram Shastri and Ichchharam later in the day.

"In presence of all of us, Dadasaheb has accepted your order. It won't be easy for him to revolt openly," Ram Shastri replied.

"We can't say so about Kaka. He had done that earlier and he could do it now. If he could come to the Chintamani temple with a sword in his hand, he can do that anywhere and anytime. He is blinded by his greed."

Shrimant, you are right. We have to convince Dadasaheb for his full support," Ram Shastri replied.

"I need your word, Shastribuwa. You will always protect Narayan from any harm." Madhavrao looked towards Ram Shastri and Ichchharam, as both nodded in support.

* * *

A large crowd had gathered in Theur to pay their last homage to Shrimant Madhavrao Peshwa who had breathed his last inside the Chintamani temple a day earlier. The love and respect were pouring in for him from all the corners of the Maratha empire. The corpse was given a royal bath and the brahmins were chanting the mantras for the deceased Peshwa. Incense sticks were ignited near the corpse which was decorated with flowers and put on a platform inside the mansion. One could hear the wailing sounds everywhere; it seemed that the whole Maratha empire was mourning the death of the Peshwa.

"Come, Narayan. Our Madhav has gone." Raghunathrao hugged Narayanrao, they were sobbing.

"Kaka, my Dada is gone... Kaka," Narayanrao was inconsolable. Gangabai came and stood next to Narayanrao and waited for the right opportunity to speak.

"She is not listening to anyone Swari, can you please come?" Gangabai requested Narayanrao who immediately understood the gravity of the situation and walked to the women's chamber in the mansion.

"Vahinisaheb, please don't do this. Please..." Ramabai was dressed in a white cotton saree, a golden necklace on her neck.

Her hair were properly tied back with a half-moon-shaped *bindi* on her forehead.

"Narayan, your brother had declared you the next Peshwa and you are crying like a child. Now it is in your hands to run the empire," Ramabai said to him. She was calm and expressionless. It seemed that she had been relieved of all the pains she had faced in the last few months.

"You can't do this, Vahinisaheb. You can't go like this." Narayanrao pleaded with her.

"It is my duty to follow my husband Narayan and please do not stop me," saying this Ramabai walked out of the women's chamber and sat near the corpse of Madhavrao.

Madhavrao's body was lifted and the procession started moving towards the Mula Mutha river, Theur was packed with people who had travelled from across the Maratha empire to see their Peshwa one last time. Ramabai was following her husband.

"Vahinisaheb, Narayan needs you. Is it necessary?"Ram Shastri tried one last time; he was a staunch opponent of *sati* practice.

"Shastribuwa, Swari has given you a big responsibility. Our Narayan is in your hands now," replied Ramabai. She removed her golden bangle and handed it to Ram Shastri.

A large wooden platform was created on the shore of the river for the last rites of Madhavrao. A stack of sandal wood was lying near it. Madhavrao's body was kept on the wooden platform and surrounded by sandal wood. An emotional crowd was in shock, but Ramabai was oblivious to all the pain of the public. She had no attachments left for worldly affairs.

Ramabai folded her hands in the direction of the Chintamani temple and said a prayer. She then touched the feet of her husband

and walked onto the platform. With a smile on her face, Ramabai sat on the platform next to her husband's corpse.

Narayanrao ignited the funeral pyre which soon spread through the sandal wood and engulfed Ramabai and Madhavrao. Theur had witnessed the biggest crowd in its history. Everyone in the crowd had teary eyes.

Marathas had lost their king, their protector, their *swami*.

NARAYANRAO'S CORONATION

The Untimely death of Madhavrao Peshwa had left a void in the empire. It was difficult to fill the footsteps of a Peshwa who was equally revered by his friends and enemies. As Narayanrao had two elder brothers, he would have never thought of becoming Peshwa. However, fate played cruelly and he lost both his brothers at an early age. Two weeks later, after performing the last rites of his brother and completing the religious rituals in Theur, Narayanrao was back in Poona.

"Shrimant, we have to go to Satara to get the robes of Peshwa for you." Nana Phadnis and Sakharam Bapu were present in Narayanrao's chamber.

"You are right, Nana. Dada is gone. Now the affairs of the state have to be taken care of!" replied Narayanrao.

"I agree, Shrimant. The musnud should not remain empty. When should we plan to go to Satara?" asked Sakharam Bapu.

"As all the last rituals for Dada have been completed, we should plan to go at the earliest," confirmed Narayanrao.

"Shrimant, since your mother is not here, I suggest that as the eldest member of the family, Dadasaheb should join you on this journey," Sakharam Bapu suggested.

"It is a good suggestion, Bapu. I will personally request Kaka to accompany us to Satara and be with us when we receive the robes of Peshwa," replied Narayanrao.

Sakharam was eyeing the post of Karbhari, but he was not sure if Narayanrao would assign him the job, so he played his card smartly.

* * *

"Dadasaheb, Shrimant is planning to go to Satara to get the robes of Peshwa," Sakharam Bapu went to meet Raghunathrao immediately after his discussion with Narayanrao.

"Let him go, he has been declared the next Peshwa," Raghunathrao replied.

"I have advised him that he should take you along," said Sakharam Bapu with a cunning smile on his face.

"I have no interest in going with Narayan or being a part of his coronation ceremony, Bapu." Raghunathrao could not decipher the diplomatic words of Sakharam Bapu.

"Dadasaheb, staying away from the administrative affairs will not help us. To keep your hold on the state activities, you have to remain a part of all the affairs," Sakharam Bapu said cunningly, he wanted to use the position of Raghunathrao to safeguard his interests.

"I am not a part of anything, Bapu. Narayan has still not appointed his ministers. I don't know what he has in his mind."

"This is the chance when you can force him to appoint Karbharis of your choice. I am sure Ram Shastri will remain the Chief justice and that anyway would not help us much."

The incident at Theur had been a setback for Raghunathrao. He had plans of overthrowing Madhavrao and taking power by force. His supporters were surrounded and he had to surrender to the wishes of Madhavrao. On his death bed, When Madhavrao declared Narayan as his successor, there was sympathy for Narayanrao. With a heavy heart, Raghunathrao had accepted the decision.

"Thank you, Bapu, for informing me about this. I will talk to Narayan."

"Shrimant Madhavrao had removed me from the post of Karbhari in his initial years." Sakharam Bapu shared his concern. Sakharam Bapu was worried that Narayanrao too, like his brother, will ignore him so he decided to take Raghunathrao's support.

"I remember Bapu, but it won't happen this time," Raghunathrao assured him.

* * *

"Kaka, I have come to make a request to you," Narayanrao went to the chamber of Raghunathrao to talk to him before leaving for Satara.

"Please tell me, Narayan. I will be happy to be of any service to you," Raghunathrao replied politely.

"I am planning to go to Satara to get the robes of Peshwa from Chhatrapati. Being the eldest member of the family here in Poona, I request you to join me on this journey. I want your presence and blessings when I get the robes from Chhatrapati." Narayanrao requested his uncle.

"Narayan, my blessings are always with you, but I won't be able to come to Satara," replied Raghunathrao. Narayanrao was not expecting this.

"Kaka, have I done anything wrong?" Narayanrao was irked.

"You have not assigned ministers here and you want to go to Satara along with me. Who will take care of Poona?" Raghunathrao questioned Narayanrao.

"I understand, Kaka. I will assign the administrative roles tomorrow and then we will go together," assured Narayanrao.

"I have a condition, Narayan." Raghunathrao tried to play his tactics.

"Kaka, if you would have said this in darbar, I would have rejected it straight away. Here I have come to you as your nephew, you can ask anything," Narayanrao spoke calmly to his uncle.

"I want Sakharam Bapu to be Karbhari when you take charge."

Raghunathrao put forward his condition. Narayanrao did not commit anything at that time and told Raghunathrao that he would give it a thought. After consulting Ram Shastri and Nana Phadnis, Narayanrao declared that Sakharam Bapu and Nana Phadnis would be appointed as Karbharis. The decision made Raghunathrao happy, and he went to Satara with Narayanrao.

The memories of Madhavrao were still fresh in the minds of Maratha chiefs, generals and the public. Therefore, the coronation celebrations were curtailed. The robes of Peshwa for Narayanrao had arrived from Satara and the coronation ceremony was planned with minimal celebrations at the Ganpati Rang Mahal.

"You have a big responsibility tomorrow, Shastribuwa." Nana Phadnis was with Ram Shastri at his house.

"I am worried about the future of the empire, Nana. It won't be easy for Shrimant Narayanrao to work with Dadasaheb."

"I understand, Shastribuwa. It is our responsibility that we keep our eyes and ears open all the time." Nana Phadnis responded.

"I have seen Dadasaheb for so many years now. I feel that this time he won't settle for the role of a regent."

"Let us not worry too much about that. All the preparations for tomorrow's ceremony are complete, it is an important day for the empire."

"You know how much he admired Shrimant Madhavrao. He misses him and unnecessarily worries about Shrimant Narayanrao," Janaki joined the discussion.

"His concern is valid, Vahinisaheb. Things will not be the same at Shaniwar Wada. It would be difficult to fulfill the footsteps of Shrimant Madhavrao." Nana responded.

They talked for a while about administrative affairs and then Nana Phadnis left for his house.

Shaniwar Wada was busy next day, for the coronation ceremony. All the dignitaries and Maratha chiefs had arrived in Poona. It was a cold December morning, and the Maratha palace was buzzing with activity.

"You are looking very happy today. After all, you got a chance to become regent to the Peshwa for the second time!" Anandibai made a sarcastic comment at Raghunathrao, who was getting ready to attend the coronation ceremony.

Anandibai was ready for the ceremony with her *nauvari* green sari draped and tucked perfectly onto her waist. A golden band was hanging from her waist and the half-moon-shaped bindi was beautifully sitting on her forehead.

"Narayan is like a son to me." Raghunathrao could not get the sarcasm and replied.

"He might be like a son to you, but he is not your son. I feel bad for you. God gave you a chance, twice, to become Peshwa, but you never grabbed the opportunities that came your way."

"I have all the power I need and I will run the affairs of the empire the way I want." Raghunathrao was confident that he would dominate the state affairs under young Narayanrao as Peshwa.

"You may get to run the affairs of the state as you want, but you won't be the Peshwa. You will remain his advisor only. Also, you had similar plans when Madhav became Peshwa, but what happened? Madhav took the charge and all the power away from you and put you under house arrest."

"Narayan is not Madhav, Anandi..." Raghunathrao was not willing to engage in the discussion; he was not very happy with the coronation of Narayanrao. Somewhere deep in his heart, the ambition to become Peshwa was still alive.

"Yes, Narayan is not Madhav. Madhav respected you for your valour and the battles you had won. He always wanted you to be part of his plans. Narayan would be worse than Madhav for you."

"You are unnecessarily worried. I will take care of everything. Now let us go to darbar, and not get late." A frustrated Raghunathrao walked out of his chamber to the darbar, oblivious to the fact that the happenings of the darbar would only make his day worse.

* * *

"No one can change whatever has happened, but now you have to lead the empire," Gangabai told Narayanrao.

Narayanrao was in his chamber and was gazing out of the window at the city. Soon, he would be in charge of the empire his elder brother had been in charge of up until a few weeks prior. The Peshwas had always flown the banner of Chhatrapati Shivaji high, and the Marathas had an illustrious heritage. "I am missing

Dada. I wish he and aai were here with me today," Narayanrao said in a soft voice. The enormous responsibility of leading the empire was a big burden on the shoulders of a young Peshwa who was concerned about his future and that of the Marathas.

"Go and join the ceremony. Everybody in the darbar would be waiting for you. You are the son of Nanasaheb Peshwa and I am confident that you would be as successful as your father and brother were." Gangabai comforted him and checked his pagdi one last time. She then cleaned his face with a soft muslin cloth. Narayanrao walked out of his chamber and Gangabai followed him with guards by their side.

All the dignitaries present in the darbar were anxiously waiting for the arrival of Narayanrao. Their minds were shrouded with doubts. Narayanrao would officially become the Peshwa, but that would not bury the family dispute to control the empire. The Bhat family had dominated the affairs of the Maratha empire for more than half a century by then and all the predecessors of Narayanrao were either good rulers or good warriors. In some cases, they were both. As Narayanrao entered the darbar, all present there stood to pay respect to the new Peshwa. Ram Shastri came forward and stood near Narayanrao.

"Shrimant, as the Chief Justice, it is my honour to walk you to the musnud," Ram Shastri said with pride.

"Shastribuwa, I would need your support and support of other senior ministers to run the empire," Narayanrao said. Together, both were walking towards the musnud.

"I am always committed to support this seat of Marathas, Shrimant. So are other ministers present here," Ram Shastri said.

Narayanrao came close to the musnud and folded his hand in front of it. He then bowed in respect before sitting on the musnud, thus becoming the fifth Peshwa of Marathas from the Bhat family.

"I, Ram Shastri Vishwasnath Prabhune, declare Shrimant Narayanrao Balaji Bhat as next Peshwa of Maratha empire and Raghunathrao Bajirao Bhat as his regent," Ram Shastri officially announced the coronation of Narayanrao.

Anandibai was sitting on the first floor of the darbar, observing the proceedings of the ceremony with jealousy in her eyes. Gangabai was sitting next to her, observing her husband taking charge of the empire with pride.

"Dadasaheb, I request you to perform the first salute to Shrimant Narayanrao," Ram Shastri requested Raghunathrao to bow in front of Narayanrao. Raghunathrao was stunned by the sudden request, and he did not move from his place. Ram Shastri found himself in a difficult situation in the darbar. If Raghunathrao would not listen to him and not pay respect to Narayanrao now, it would weaken the position of the new Peshwa in the eyes of all the dignitaries.

"Dadasaheb, as the regent to the Peshwa, it is you who should do the first salute. This is to the seat of Maratha empire," Ram Shastri requested again.

Raghunathrao was visibly upset. He was asked to bow down to Narayanrao, which he could not bear. Anandibai was annoyed by the proceedings. All present in the darbar were expectantly looking at Ram Shastri. No one had been expecting this drama. Ram Shastri looked towards Nana Phadnis, who came forward to his rescue.

"Dadasaheb, all present here in this darbar are aware of your commitment to the Maratha empire. This salute is just to reiterate the same commitment and loyalty," Nana Phadnis said diplomatically.

Raghunathrao sensed that he could not openly oppose Narayanrao's coronation in full darbar. He came forward and stood in front of Narayanrao, who was sitting on the throne. Raghunathrao looked around, all the eyes in the darbar were on him. This would be the ultimate humiliation for life, he felt. Raghunathrao looked in the direction where Anandibai was sitting. Her eyes were burning with rage and her ego was badly hurt. Hurriedly, Raghunathrao bowed and saluted to the new Peshwa before taking his seat. Anandibai felt so humiliated that she rushed out of the darbar.

The proceedings of the darbar ended in sometime and Narayanrao went to his chamber along with Ram Shastri.

"Shastribuwa, is this the way one should behave in darbar?" Narayanrao asked Ram Shastri.

"Shrimant, we should be patient with Dadasaheb. He has his way of working. I agree with you that the seat of Peshwa should be respected by one and all," replied Ram Shastri.

"How will I work if Kaka will behave like this?" Narayanrao said thoughtfully and took a deep breath.

"You will find a way to work with Dadasaheb, Shrimant. I would suggest you try to strengthen your relationship with him on a personal level."

"How can I do that, Shastribuwa? Kaka doesn't want to talk to me. He treats me like a child."

"When one doesn't listen in the matters of politics, you have to take the personal matters in your hands." Gangabai entered the chamber and joined the discussion.

"What are you suggesting, Ganga?" asked Narayanrao.

"Your sister, Durgabai, is of marriageable age. You should help Kaka in finding the right match and arrange the marriage." Gangabai made the suggestion. Both Narayanrao and Ram Shastri were impressed by her advice.

"I liked this idea, Shastribuwa. We have to search for the right match for our Durga. Do you have any match in your mind for Durgabai?"

"I do. Shrimant, first you have to discuss this with Dadasaheb to gauge his feelings," Ram Shastri responded.

Baramati was an old town that was ruled by Marathas at the start of the seventeenth century, but later it was controlled by Mughals. After the death of the Aurangzeb in 1707, the influence of Mughals slowly declined and Marathas gained supremacy. Baramati again came under the Maratha empire. It was in 1745 when Shahu Maharaj handed the administration of Baramati to Babuji Naik Joshi, who was a Peshwa Sardar and a loyalist.

Babuji Naik had come to Poona to attend the coronation ceremony and was going to stay in Poona for a few days. A personal invitation had been sent by Peshwa to invite Babuji Naik for dinner.

"Come, Kaka. I wanted to discuss something personal with you." Narayanrao had also invited Raghunathrao for the dinner with him and Babuji Naik.

"Have you called me to discuss what happened in the darbar yesterday?" Raghunathrao asked in a concerned voice.

"No, Kaka. I have called you to discuss something more important. Durga came to meet me yesterday evening to wish me. You know how fond I am of her as she is the only sister I have. Yesterday I felt a very strong affection for her. When I talked to her, I realized that she has grown up so fast. I have called you to talk about her."

"What about Durga?" Raghunathrao had no clue where the discussion was headed and he felt relieved that Narayanrao was not talking about any political matter.

"She is of marriageable age now, Kaka. I think we should try to find a good match for her. As her elder brother, and now the Peshwa of the empire, it is my duty to find a suitable match for my sister." Narayanrao spoke with affection.

"I am happy to hear this from you, Narayan. It takes a burden off my shoulders." Raghunathrao smiled hearing the statement of his nephew.

"I have found a suitable match for her and have planned a dinner today which I want you to join. I am sure you won't have any objection." Narayanrao took the consent of his Kaka. In a rare show of bonhomie, both had the same opinion on the matter.

A servant announced the arrival of special guests. Narayanrao went to the entrance of his chamber to welcome Babuji Naik who was accompanied by Sakharam Bapu. Narayanrao offered the royal dinner to his guests before initiating the topic of a marriage alliance.

* * *

Narayanrao, along with Gangabai, personally took charge of all the preparations for the marriage of Durgabai. It was important for the new Peshwa to develop a strong bond with his uncle and this was his best chance. In the last few years, Narayanrao had developed a strong affection for his cousin sister, and post the death of Madhavrao, his relationship with Durgabai only strengthened.

When the marriage alliance was proposed by Narayanrao to Babuji Naik in the presence of Raghunathrao, it was immediately accepted. Babuji Naik agreed to take Durgabai as a bride for his son Pandurangrao and he requested an early marriage. After discussing with the royal priest, a suitable date was finalized. They had only a few weeks to make all the preparations for the marriage.

"Nana, I hope that all the arrangements for the stay of guests are complete." Narayanrao was with Nana Phadnis on a visit to the Parvati temple.

"Shrimant, all the preparations are complete. It would be a grand wedding ceremony," Nana Phadnis replied.

"Hope the menu for the guests had been finalized and Kaka had given his consent for it."

"Yes, Shrimant. Dadasaheb had checked all the preparations for the royal lunch for the guests and approved. All the dishes are personally selected by Vahinisaheb," replied Nana Phadnis. Narayanrao was happy that Gangabai was also supporting him.

"Shrimant, some more invitations are pending," Nana Phadnis told Narayanrao, who took the list from him and planned to write all the invitation letters on the same day. Narayanrao was busy writing the invitation letters when a servant announced the arrival of Raghunathrao and Anandibai.

"Narayan, you seem to have been very busy for the last few days," Raghunathrao asked him.

"Kaka, please come. I am personally writing the invitation letters to all the guests. I have just dispatched a letter to Tukoji Holkar," replied Narayanrao.

"I am so happy to see that you have taken charge of all the preparations for the marriage. I am happy that all the work is being done to perfection."

"It is my duty, Kaka."

"I know we are facing financial difficulties at this moment, but still, you have been very large-hearted to arrange a grand ceremony for Durga."

"Kaka, Durga is the Peshwa's sister. She deserves this grand ceremony. Also, I am sure soon the financial situation of the state will improve," Narayanrao replied. The empty treasury had been a big concern for him since he had taken charge.

The fireworks and decoration of the city were planned well in advance and specially-skilled craftsmen had travelled from far off places. The streets of the city and the courtyard of the palaces were cleaned on daily basis and light water was spread. The outer area was layered with cow dung and rangoli was made in the inner parts. Decorative lanterns and festoons made of multi-coloured paper and artificial flowers of paper and wax were used to decorate the entrance, along with the natural plants placed symmetrically near fountains.

As the guests arrived, *gandha*, a mark on the forehead made of sandalwood paste and saffron, was applied by special servants who were neatly dressed in uniforms. Various types of *attars* were arranged and applied to each guest as per their taste and choice.

The meal arrangements were done as per the tastes of Maratha allies from various parts of the kingdom. A special menu with over fifty items was prepared. Many types of *pan-vidas* were also prepared for the royal guests.

The marriage ceremony was held in the Ganpati Rang Mahal of Shaniwar Wada. The royal priests read the mantras as the marriage ritual continued.

"Sasubai, our Durga is looking so beautiful." Gangabai was standing with Anandibai.

"I didn't realize when she had grown up," Anandibai replied with tears in her eyes.

The festivities continued at Shaniwar Wada. The marriage ceremony of Durgabai was sure to be remembered by generations.

A day after the marriage ceremony, Raghunathrao and Anandibai walked to the chamber of Narayanrao to thank him.

"Kaka..." Narayanrao was pleasantly surprised to see them in his chamber. Raghunathrao did not say anything; he went ahead and hugged Narayanrao.

The bonhomie between the two was at full display.

THE HOUSE ARREST

6

"Times have changed at Shaniwar Wada, Bapu. Still, nothing has changed for me," said Visajipant Lele. Raghunathrao had gained power in the reign of Narayanrao and many of his loyalists were approaching him to get back their lost glory and position of power.

"I will talk to Dadasaheb and will put forward your request in the darbar. I don't think there should be any problem in reinstating you," Sakharam Bapu told Visajipant Lele. They were on their way to Shaniwar Wada.

"Do you think Narayanrao will agree to this?"

"If Dadasaheb will recommend, Narayanrao will have no option, but to agree!"

"I attended Durgabai's marriage and have seen the bonhomie between the two. However, some time has passed since then and I think their relation is no more the same," Visajipant responded.

"Nothing has changed, Visaji. Dadasaheb is controlling all the affairs of the empire and there is nothing to worry about. You meet me in the darbar later today." Sakharam Bapu assured him and went to meet Raghunathrao.

"Dadasaheb, Visajipant is here to meet you," Sakharam Bapu tried to arrange a meeting for Visajipant.

"What does he want?" Raghunathrao asked.

"He has done so much for the empire, but he was treated like a criminal in the court of Marathas. Visajipant has always been your supporter, Dadasaheb. If you support him now, his services could be of use for us in the future."

"That was a different time, Bapu. Now things have changed. I will certainly put forward his case."

"Yes, Dadasaheb. Now you are in power and things have changed. I know if you would speak to Shrimant, he could easily get his position back." Bapu suggested.

"Narayanrao is taking too much advice from Ram Shastri these days, but I will take this up on the darbar today itself."

"I know Ram Shastri. Even if Shrimant agrees to this, it would be difficult to convince Ram Shastri. He had given his judgement long ago."

"Let us go to darbar, Bapu. Let me see who stops me from doing what I want to do," Raghunathrao said authoritatively.

When he arrived, the darbar was getting ready to start. Narayanrao had entered and taken his seat. He was not in a good mood. After waiting for some time, Raghunathrao signalled to Sakharam Bapu to talk about Visajipant Lele.

"Shrimant, I have a request to the darbar today," Sakharam Bapu rose from his seat and requested Narayanrao.

"Please go ahead, Bapu," Narayanrao responded calmly.

"Visajipant Lele has done great service to the Maratha empire. He has not only won many battles for Marathas, but also kept a watch on the British and their plans. He even helped us to foil many advances made by them. I know he has committed some mistakes in the past, but his service to the empire is of far high value. He has already paid for his mistakes."

"Come to the point, Bapu. I don't understand what you want to convey," Narayanrao was irked by the request; he was aware of the crimes of Visajipant.

"Shrimant, we have Visajipant here with us in the darbar and he has a request to the Peshwa. He should be reinstated to the post of Governor of Bassein." Sakharam Bapu tried to use his authority in the darbar to press Peshwa for a favourable order.

"You are right, Bapu. Considering the service of Visajipant, he should be made Governor of Bassein again." Raghunathrao put his weight behind the request made by Sakharam Bapu. Ram Shastri was keenly listening to the request made by them.

"Kaka, that decision is to be made by the Peshwa," Narayanrao said curtly.

"Yes, Shrimant. We request you to kindly consider our request to reinstate Visajipant," Sakharam Bapu added.

"Visajipant had been removed from the post of Governor for a reason," Ram Shastri joined the conversation.

Sakharam Bapu was expecting this resistance from Ram Shastri. He looked towards Raghunathrao who too seemed unhappy by his comment.

"Shastribuwa, anyone can make mistakes, but if someone is ready to correct their mistakes, he should be forgiven," Raghunathrao commented.

"Dadasaheb, you are trivializing the act of cheating the royal treasury as a mistake," Ram Shastri shot back at Raghunathrao.

"It depends on how we look at things, Shastribuwa. This darbar has already trivialized his services and the work he did for the empire. He committed one mistake, and he was treated like the enemy of Marathas." Raghunathrao was not happy with the proceedings of the darbar. He rose from his seat and paced around the darbar.

"Visajipant is a corrupt person who was involved in many illegal practices. He had cheated the state of a few lacs which he collected, but did not deposit in the royal treasury. Shrimant Madhavrao Peshwa had given him the punishment he deserved in this darbar only. Justice had already been delivered." Ram Shastri spoke with confidence and authority.

"Matter of justice is different from the matter of politics, Shastribuwa. We need committed and royal soldiers like him to run the affairs of the state. If we start punishing all our loyalists for their small mistakes, we won't have anyone standing with us to fight the battles," Raghunathrao reasoned in the darbar, went closer to Visajipant, and patted him on the shoulder.

"We don't need corrupt soldiers like him, Kaka. Dada had already decided in this darbar what should be done and his decision would not be changed. Shastribuwa is the judge of the empire and he had also shared his views on Visajipant," Narayanrao declared.

"But Narayan..."

"Our decision is final; we won't change what Dada had already decided." Narayanrao stood from his seat and said in a loud voice. Raghunathrao could not even complete his sentence.

It was an embarrassing moment for Raghunathrao; his request was straightaway rejected in full darbar and he had to take back his words.

Visajipant Lele was the Governor of Bassein. He was a soldier of merit and had fought many battles for Marathas. But he was also a shrewd and greedy person. On many occasions, he had not only wrongfully attacked and looted British ships, but also did not deposit the loot in the royal treasury. When this was brought to the attention of Madhavrao Peshwa, he fined him and removed him from his post. Visajipant was close to Raghunathrao and Sakharam Bapu. Within a few months of Madhavrao's death, he approached them to get his post back.

Narayanrao was slowly asserting his control and on most occasions his thoughts differed from that of his uncle. Raghunathrao tried to intervene in state affairs and Narayanrao was not happy with the constant interference by his uncle. When Raghunathrao tried to intervene again in the case of Visajipant, it irked Narayanrao, who took a stand and stood firm with the decision taken by his deceased brother and Ram Shastri.

The power was shifting again and Raghunathrao felt threatened. He was losing control of the Maratha empire to a much younger Narayanrao.

* * *

"What happened Chinto, you have come alone?" Raghunathrao was eagerly waiting for Chinto Vitthal in his chamber.

"There was a problem, Dadasaheb." Chinto Vitthal responded.

"You can't even get a *batik* on time!" Raghunathrao responded angrily.

"I had bought a batik. While coming to Shaniwar Wada, we met Ram Shastri on the way and that batik begged him for help."

"Why are you telling me stories Chinto?" Raghunathrao said sarcastically.

"It is not a story, Dadasaheb. I am telling you the truth. That batik rushed to the house of Ram Shastri and pleaded for help."

"What did Ram Shastri do then?" questioned Raghunathrao.

"He took her in and closed the door on us."

"How can he do that? Let us go to his house right now." Raghunathrao was frowning with anger as Ram Shastri was becoming a constant obstacle in his plans.

"There is no point in going to his house. Ram Shastri told us that he would be coming to darbar soon." Chinto stopped him.

"Let us go to darbar then. This Raghoba has not become so helpless that he can't even purchase a batik," Raghunathrao thundered and rushed out of his chamber.

As Raghunathrao and Chinto Vitthal entered the darbar, they saw Ram Shastri coming from the other side with a young woman who had dishevelled hair and torn clothes. All present in the darbar were shocked to see a woman in such a state. Narayanrao got up from his seat and walked towards Ram Shastri.

A dasi came forward with a cloth to cover the woman.

"There is no need to do that, let the darbar also see how women are treated in the Maratha empire." Ram Shastri stopped the dasi from covering the woman.

"What is this, Shastribuwa?" Narayanrao was puzzled by the presence of a woman who entered the darbar with Ram Shastri.

"I also have the same question, Shrimant. What is this going on in the empire?" Ram Shastri responded, pointing his finger toward the woman.

"Shastribuwa, you come to the darbar with a woman in such a state and instead of answering my question, you are asking me a question?" Narayanrao countered Ram Shastri.

"If you want to know about the state of this helpless woman, then you ask Dadasaheb! But if you want to know why she has come with me to the court, then I can answer."

"Shastribuwa, Chinto told me that you had snatched our batik from him," Raghunathrao spoke.

"Shrimant, this batik here wants to ask some questions to the Peshwa. She wants to know whether the rules made for humans in this empire apply to her or not? She wants to know what crime she has committed that in full bazaar she was treated and traded like an animal?" Ram Shastri ignored the question asked by Raghunathrao and talked to Narayanrao.

"Shastribuwa, a human is always treated as a human in our empire," Narayanrao responded.

"Forgive me, Shrimant. But in that case, you have not seen all the activities of your empire. Every week in Poona, these women are bought and sold in an open market. People gather around them, put a price on them, then pay the money and take them away. Isn't that how an animal is traded? What is the difference between the two? Is being a woman a crime in this city?"

"But this practice of slave trade is going on for a long time Shastribuwa, and it is legal," Narayanrao replied.

"Shastribuwa, Narayan is correct. This is legal and being the judge of the Marathas, you must know this rule. Today you have committed a crime by snatching a batik from Chinto. We have bought her from the market and as per rule, she should be with the person who has purchased her," Raghunathrao said cunningly and tried to undermine the Chief Justice.

"You are right, Dadasaheb. I have committed a crime here. As per the rule, slave trade is legal and thus this batik here belongs to her owner. Shrimant, as a part of the Maratha empire, she has some hopes from the Peshwa. She expects to be treated like a human. Just because someone is poor, we can't treat them like animals. If the rule says we can mistreat humans and trade them, then we must change that rule. A rule is for the people. People are not for the rule. As a society, we have to change with changing times." Ram Shastri argued in the darbar and fearlessly challenged the Peshwa.

"But till the time the rule remains, we have all the rights to take that batik with us. Chinto, take that batik," Raghunathrao ordered.

"Shastribuwa, please help," the batik fell on the feet of Ram Shastri and pleaded.

"I am sorry Kamla, this full-court of Marathas can't do anything for a helpless woman," Ram Shastri intentionally made that comment, addressing the batik by her first name and trying to move away from her.

"Stop, Chinto! Shastribuwa, you are the judge and you have to suggest how can we help her?" Narayanrao asked Ram Shastri. The trick had worked.

"Dadasaheb is right in buying a batik as it is legal and allowed as per the rule. If we want to help this woman, we have to change the rules. Shrimant Madhavrao was against slave trade and he once ordered to stop slave trade, but, as there is no written record of that, we can't argue on that order. As the Peshwa of the empire, you have all the rights to issue an order on official paper with the royal seal and ban slave trade."

A servant was sent to get the official paper from the treasury along with the royal seal. He handed it to Ram Shastri, who wrote the order to ban slave trade with immediate effect. Then he put the royal seal on it and handed it to Narayanrao to sign. Narayan looked at the woman, who was still sitting on the floor near Ram Shastri, and signed the order to ban slave trade in the Maratha empire.

"Kamla, from today onwards, no one in the Maratha empire would be able to buy or sell a woman," Narayanrao declared in the court.

Ram Shastri looked at the order signed by the Peshwa; he was happy that his efforts for banning slave trade since the time of Madhavrao Peshwa had yielded some results. Narayanrao Peshwa went back to his seat, Kamla got up from the floor, bowed with folded hands in front of the Peshwa, and thanked him for his kind gesture.

"I don't understand what is going on here! Chinto, get hold of that batik and bring her to our chamber," Raghunathrao ordered Chinto.

He paid no heed to the announcement made by the Peshwa. A stunned batik started trembling as Chinto approached her and got hold of her arm. Terrified, she looked towards the Peshwa for help.

"Chinto, mind your acts in the darbar of the Peshwa. An order has been passed and any act against the order would be treated as an act against the empire and will be tried in court as treason." Narayanrao thundered in the court.

"Orders are not passed like this, Narayan. There should be some discussion with experienced ministers," Raghunathrao tried to object.

"An order has been passed, Kaka. If you defy this, you too would be tried for treason. Mind your words when you speak in the darbar against the Peshwa." Narayanrao responded to his uncle, who was shocked to hear such a harsh reply.

Raghunathrao did not say anything further. He signalled Chinto to leave the batik and follow him. Narayanrao sent Kamla to Gangabai.

The relationship between Narayanrao and his uncle was continuously deteriorating and the mutual respect was missing between the two. Gopikabai was following the happenings of Shaniwar Wada from Gangapur. She sensed danger to her son from Raghunathrao. She wrote to Narayanrao that there was a chance that Raghunathrao may openly revolt and strict actions should be taken in advance to counter any such act. Narayanrao was in dilemma whether he should discuss this with Sakharam Bapu or not, as he was a close aid of Raghunathrao.

As Madhavrao had done earlier, when left with no options, Narayanrao too did the same. To counter any revolt, Raghunathrao was put under house arrest on the orders of the Peshwa.

It was the beginning of a nasty conflict between the Peshwa and his uncle.

* * *

"Shrimant, Dadasaheb is an elder member of the family and he is your uncle. Such strict terms of house arrest for him would only make things worse." Ram Shastri was sitting with Narayanrao in his chamber a few days after the house arrest order.

"Shastribuwa, Kaka has not left us with any option. He had openly revolted against Dada and I fear that he can openly revolt against us also. You remember a few months back when we went to Gangapur to meet aaosaheb, Kaka left Shaniwar Wada and camped on the outskirts of the city. He even tried to gather troops with the support of his loyalists."

"There is no doubt that Dadasaheb is capable of a revolt, but making his life difficult would not reduce the risk of a coup; it will only make him more desperate for revolt. This way he would garner sympathy also."

"Kaka is desperate for a coup for over a decade now, Shastribuwa. He has to be controlled. I am not sure if this is the right way, but something had to be done immediately, so this order of house arrest."

"Forgive me, Shrimant, but Dadasaheb should be allowed some visitors. I met Bapu today and he told me that even he is not allowed to meet Dadasaheb."

"I wrote to aaosaheb, and she suggested that Kaka should be put under house arrest with strict conditions and should not be allowed any visitors." Narayanrao shared the main reason why he had put Raghunathrao under strict house arrest.

"Shrimant, you know the reasons why Matoshri had left Poona forever. The affairs of the state are performed with political wisdom and not by the instructions of loved ones." Ram Shastri responded.

Gopikabai had a strong influence on Madhavrao and tried to guide him on state affairs. When differences arose between mother and son on the matter of her brother and Madhavrao did not listen to her, she left Poona forever. As Narayanrao took charge of Peshwai, she started guiding him on various matters of state. She had political wisdom and knowledge, but also had her own biases. The strongest one she had was against her cousin, Anandibai.

Ram Shastri was aware of the interference Gopikabai had during the reign of Madhavrao and was surprised to see that though she was not in Poona for years, she was still trying to interfere in state matters. The two key members of the Peshwa family, Raghunathrao and Narayanrao, were slowly drifting apart from each other and this was apparent in the proceedings of the darbar.

"What should I do, Shastribuwa? Sometimes I feel alone in the palace which houses thousands of people. I feel everyone in the palace wants me to fail. I can't trust anyone anymore. I feel there is no one who I can look up to for the right advice," Narayanrao shared his emotions with Ram Shastri.

"Shrimant, I am always there at your service as and when you need me. You need not feel alone. I understand that fate has been cruel to you, but you have to be strong to serve the empire."

"You suggest Shastribuwa, what should I do with Kaka?"

"House arrest is nothing new for Dadasaheb. He was kept under house arrest earlier also, but Shrimant Madhavrao knew the limits and respected the personal needs of your Kaka. It would be good if Dadasaheb is allowed some visitors."

"If you suggest so, I will immediately remove the restrictions."

"I feel that a blunder had already been committed in the case of the Prabhu community episode which had dented your image. At this stage, putting Dadasaheb under such conditions would only help him get sympathy from various sections." Ram Shastri concluded.

As the Peshwa removed the restrictions on visitors to Raghunathrao, Ram Shastri himself went to inform him about the orders and to understand his state of mind at the time.

"You look very weak, Dadasaheb. How is your health?" Ram Shastri asked Raghunathrao.

"I am happy to see that you are concerned about my health, Shastribuwa." Raghunathrao was in his chamber.

"I have requested Shrimant to allow visitors to meet you in person in your chamber."

"What is my mistake that I am treated like an enemy of the Peshwa? I deserve to live with honour. I would happily retire and go on a pilgrimage," Raghunathrao questioned philosophically.

"Both of us can go to pilgrimage together Dadasaheb." Ram Shastri comforted him.

"I need your help, Shastribuwa. I would like to meet Bapu; can you please send my message to him?"

"Dadasaheb, I will pass your message. As you know that Ganeshotsav is starting next week. I want you to join the celebrations with Shrimant at Ganpati Rang Mahal." Ram Shastri tried to read the mind of Raghunathrao and persuade him to be part of the celebrations.

"I will not be a part of any royal celebrations, Shastribuwa. I am a prisoner of the state," Raghunathrao responded.

Ram Shastri talked to him for a while and then left his chamber. On his way, he reluctantly arranged to send a message to Sakharam Bapu.

Narayanrao had come to his chamber from the darbar and had not spoken anything for long. He was standing near the window and staring at the city. Gangabai, who was eagerly waiting for him to say something, sensed his mood. Kamla was there in the chamber and was preparing the room, Gangabai instructed her to leave.

"You look upset today," Gangabai broke the silence, she walked slowly towards her husband and stood close to him.

"I wrote to aaoshaeb and she has responded. I don't know how to follow her instructions."

"There are many people here in the darbar you can consult before taking a decision."

"There are many people to consult in the darbar, but somehow these days, most of the time, I feel alone Ganga."

"Don't say that..." Ganga took his hand in her hands and kept it on her belly and blushed.

"What is the matter, Ganga?" Narayanrao was puzzled by the intimate act of his wife.

"Soon, you won't be alone then," she said softly and blushed again.

"Really?" Narayanrao was excited.

"Yes, soon you will become a father." Gangabai smiled.

Narayanrao turned to Gangabai and hugged her; his eyes were wet.

It was after a long time that Narayanrao had heard some good news. He still missed his brother, Madhavrao.

"If it is a boy, we will name him Sawai Madhavrao, in the memory of Dada," Narayanrao told Gangabai and kissed her on the forehead.

THE ESCAPE PLAN

7

Preparations for the Ganeshotsav were going on and Shaniwar Wada was buzzing with activity. Sakharam Bapu had performed his administrative activities and proceeded to meet Raghunathrao. Raghunathrao was in his chamber, still under house arrest, but with limited restrictions. He was walking impatiently inside his chamber, eagerly waiting for the arrival of Sakharam Bapu.

"Bapu, I am happy that finally I could meet you," Raghunathrao was cheerful when Sakharam Bapu arrived in his chamber.

"These restrictions by Shrimant are beyond my understanding Dadasaheb. It can't go like this for long. We have to find a way out."

"Narayanrao is now Peshwa, and he has all the powers to do what he wants to do. I don't think we have any control now," Raghunathrao replied while Sakharam Bapu was listening patiently.

"You are talking like a man on the battlefield who has already assumed himself as a loser, Dadasaheb. You are the senior-most member of the family. Despite this, you have been imprisoned again and again." Sakharam Bapu replied thoughtfully touching on the sensitive topic for Raghunathrao.

"Let us change the topic, Bapu. I have called you to discuss the succession issue in Nagpur. Mudhoji is our close aid and he should get my full support. We can trust Mudhoji and we will get his support whenever required." Raghunathrao changed the topic and decided to talk about a pertinent political issue for the empire in which he had a personal stake.

"The decision is already made, Dadasaheb. Sabaji and Mudhoji both wanted to take the charge of Nagpur. I know, for us, it would be good if Mudhoji gets Nagpur, but you know the opinion of late Shrimant Madhavrao Peshwa."

"I know, but Madhav is not here anymore."

"Shrimant Narayanrao is here and the way he is taking the decisions, it is very difficult to convince him on any political matter. I have heard some rumours that the earlier proclamation of declaring Raghuji as successor might be overturned. Shrimant Narayanrao and Nana are still not very comfortable with the arrangements. This decision may not hold for long." Sakharam Bapu had his network and had learned that the succession issues of Nagpur could take a different turn in the coming days.

"That is the reason I called you here, Bapu. Make sure that Raghuji's coronation happens as early as possible. Ganeshotsav is a good time for the ceremony. Send my message to Mudhoji on this," Raghunathrao said.

"Lakshman and Vyankatrao, two agents of Mudhoji, are already in Poona to get the robes of *sena-saheb-subha* for Raghuji, but there is no progress on that matter. They are interested in meeting you also. Mudhoji is not happy with the way things are proceeding here. There is still no confirmation from Shrimant and the robes of sena-saheb-subha are still not given for Raghuji."

"When will I get a chance to meet Lakshman and Vyankatrao?" asked a curious Raghunathrao.

"I am planning to arrange a meeting, but under the current security arrangements, it is difficult. You will get a chance to meet Lakshman soon. He is a well-wisher and has expressed his wish to meet you in private. Mudhoji has also extended his support to you, Dadasaheb." Bapu confirmed.

"Arrange that meeting at the earliest with Lakshman. I have made a plan to get rid of this house arrest." Raghunathrao stopped in the middle of the sentence.

Sakharam waited for him to say more, but he did not tell anything about his plan. Sakharam understood that Raghunathrao would reveal his plan only at the right moment.

After the death of Janoji Bhosle in May 1772, the succession issue of Nagpur was ongoing for over a year now. Sabaji and Mudhoji were brothers of Janoji, who had differences in succession and were fighting with each other. Janoji had adopted Mudhoji's son at a very young age and he seemed to be the natural heir to the kingdom, but both the brothers did not agree. When the matter reached Madhavrao Peshwa, he sided with Sabaji Bhosle, but the issue remained pending. Narayanrao also followed what his brother had already decided and Nana Phadnis supported him. However, after discussions with both the brothers, much to the discomfort of Peshwa, Raghuji was declared the legal heir.

The city of Poona was getting ready to celebrate the annual Ganpati festival and the bazaar was decorated for the festival. Narayanrao was in Ganpati Rang Mahal talking to Haripant Phadke about the preparations for Ganeshotsav when Ichchharam arrived. He was gasping for breath.

"What happened, Ichchharam?" Narayanrao asked him.

"Shrimant, there is some issue at the Dilli Darwaza. Gardis have closed the gate and are not allowing anyone to enter or leave. They are not opening the gate also," Ichchharam told him.

"Shrimant, this is not the first time the Gardis are creating ruckus now and then for the last few months. I will go and check," Haripant tried to trivialize the issue.

"Haripant, we have talked about this earlier also. I want Sumer Singh to be in darbar today." Narayanrao was upset with the fact that the issues of Gardis were not resolved despite his involvement.

Haripant went to the Dilli Darwaza. A group of Gardis had surrounded it led by Sumer Singh Gardi and they had blocked all the movement through the gate. Gardis were the official security guards at Shaniwar Wada; they were mostly migrants from northern parts and devoted to their work with no political affection for any specific political faction. Gardis worked for money and protected the Shaniwar Wada for many years. In the recent past, as financial issues troubled the Maratha empire, Gardis also bore the brunt of the same.

"Sumer, is it true that Gardis are creating ruckus in Shaniwar Wada again?" Narayanrao asked Sumer Singh when he reached the darbar.

"Sarkar, we have our stomachs to feed and children to raise," replied Sumer Singh. Narayanrao did not say anything. He was aware of the financial situation of the empire. Narayanrao realized the sensitivity of the issue, but did not like the response of Sumer Singh.

"Bapu, we discussed last time that salaries of Gardis would be cleared immediately. What progress has happened in that?"

"Shrimant, you know we don't have sufficient money to pay the salaries," Sakharam Bapu replied.

"Bapu, if we can't protect those who protect Shaniwar Wada, this grand palace of Marathas, who else can we protect? I don't want to hear any excuses. I want this issue to be resolved at the earliest." Narayanrao ordered.

"Sarkar, all Gardis will be thankful to you. I will immediately order the opening of Dilli Darwaza." Sumer Singh conceded his demands.

"Sumer, I don't want any such act in the future. Your responsibility is to protect Shaniwar Wada, not to create a ruckus inside it. I order deduction of one day salary of all Gardis for today's act," Narayanrao ordered.

Sumer Singh bowed in front of the Peshwa and left the darbar in haste. Gardis were disgruntled when they heard the news of a one-day salary deduction.

Narayanrao had tried his best to resolve the issue of Gardis, but the matter was not taken up seriously by other ministers. Despite multiple reminders from the Peshwa, Sakharam Bapu did not take the cause of Gardis further. Gardis were already upset with Narayanrao and now, they were disappointed when they did not get their salaries on time despite the protests at Dilli Darwaza. To make matter worse, they were punished with salary deductions for a day.

Gardis' problems remained unresolved despite the protests.

"Did you hear what has happened in the darbar today?" Anandibai asked Tuloji.

"Yes, Vahinisaheb. I did."

"Everything is moving in the right direction. The day is not far when Swari would become Peshwa," declared Anandibai. For long she had nurtured that dream.

"What do you have in your mind?" Tuloji asked with curiosity. Anandibai calmly explained her plan to Tuloji. She trusted him completely and was sure that she needed his support to execute what she had planned.

Tuloji was shocked to hear her plan; his expression changed when he heard the full plan.

"Don't you think it would be too dangerous for Dadasaheb?" a concerned Tuloji asked.

"There is no danger in it Tuloji. We will plan carefully with minute details. The most important part here is how friendly you can get with Gardis. Just remember that Sumer Singh is your man," Anandibai told him.

Anandibai was an astute observer of the socio-political events in the empire and participated in many political conversations with her husband and regularly joined the darbar. She had a strong influence on her husband who sought her advice on various subjects. While she was making her plan, she keenly observed the Gardis and Sumer Singh, who was in charge of the security when Raghunathrao was under house arrest. She found him an influential man who had a strong hold on the Gardis. And much to her liking, he was ambitious and greedy. She decided to make him an integral part of her plans.

The rumours that Raghunathrao was planning a revolt again reached Nagpur. Mudhoji immediately dispatched his informer to Poona to convey his support for any coup planned by Raghunathrao. Mudhoji was getting jittery by the behaviour of Narayanrao, who had still not formally handed the robes of the sena-saheb-subha to the agents of Nagpur. Lakshman and his brother were keenly observing the activities at Shaniwar Wada and getting instructions from Mudhoji. When Tuloji Pawar approached Lakshman to help plan an escape for Raghunathrao, he immediately agreed, and a quick plan was made.

As suggested by Anandibai, a few days later, Lakshman was in the chamber of Raghunathrao and they were planning the escape.

"Dadasaheb, it will be my honour to be of any service to you. We have clear instructions that we must support you under any circumstances," Lakshman told Raghunathrao.

"Thank you, Lakshman. I will also take up the issue of your rights to be recognized as Kshatriya for the Prabhu community and be allowed to perform the prayers as you were doing during the time of Shivaji Maharaj."

"If you could do that, the whole Prabhu community would stand in your support. Prabhu community is already unhappy with Shrimant Narayanrao for his stand against us," Lakshman said.

"It is getting difficult to stay at Shaniwar Wada now. To make any plans and seek the support of my loyalists, I need to get out of Shaniwar Wada so that I can freely interact with my well-wishers."

"Yes, Dadasaheb. You are right. I waited for weeks to get a chance to meet you. I learned about your situation from Tuloji. We talked at length about this and have made a plan."

"Happy to hear that!"

"It is a simple plan, Dadasaheb. I have talked to Gardis. Due to the preparations for Ganeshotsav, there will be many servants going in and out of Shaniwar Wada for the next few days from early morning to late evening. There is not much checking late at night. That is when we will escape, disguised as servants."

"Seems like a good idea. When are we planning to escape?" Raghunathrao was impatient to get his freedom back.

"We will leave tonight only," Lakshman told him and shared more details with Raghunathrao, promising to come back in the evening.

"Is everything going on as per plan?" Anandibai asked Tuloji when he reached her chamber later in the evening.

"Yes, Vahinisaheb. Everything is as per plan."

"The day is not far Tuloji, when my dream will be fulfilled. You have been a big help and I have complete trust in you. Make sure that the escape plan is executed with perfection," Anandibai said enthusiastically.

"I am still not able to understand your plan. To me, it seems very dangerous. Narayanrao is very fickle minded, and it is difficult to predict what he would do. We are taking a big risk here."

"For the seat of the Peshwa, no risk is big risk Tuloji. I will tell you more about it when the time comes," Anandibai told him.

The tussle for the Peshwai in the family was going on for long and Raghunathrao had revolted openly on many occasions. But no one suspected any involvement of Anandibai in any misdeeds of her husband. She looked at the tussle with a different lens. It was she who realized that Peshwai can't be snatched with an armed revolt. It was she who realized that her husband was too emotional to give back the Peshwai even if he gets it with an armed revolt. No one in the empire, including her husband, had any idea what she was planning.

Narayanrao was sleeping in his chamber when a servant came rushing. After multiple requests, the personal guard of the Peshwa went to wake him up. It was past midnight. When the servant told the news to Narayanrao, he immediately rushed to the Dilli Darwaza where Haripant Phadke was already waiting for him.

It was dark due to which Narayanrao took a while to recognize the person standing in front of him. His hands were tied with a rope and when the guards recognized who he was, they were untying the ropes.

"Kaka?" Narayanrao was puzzled to see his uncle in that condition. Raghunathrao did not respond. Narayanrao stopped the guards who were untying the ropes. Raghunathrao was standing like a prisoner in front of the Peshwa with his hands tied.

"Shrimant, we got a tip from our informers that Dadasaheb would try to escape tonight. He was planning to escape disguised as a servant as the movement is high due to Ganeshotsav preparations and there is not much checking. Our guards were alert and they caught him." Haripant told Narayanrao.

"What do you want to achieve by doing all this, Kaka?" Narayanrao asked, but there was no response from Raghunathrao who was feeling humiliated.

"Who all were involved?" Narayanrao questioned Haripant.

"We could not catch anyone else, but our informer said that Lakshman had visited him early in the day and this was planned by him. Mudhoji from Nagpur was sending instructions to Lakshman." Haripant told Narayanrao who waited for a while and then decided to walk Raghunathrao to his chamber with his hands still tied with the ropes.

They walked in silence, closely followed by the guards. Neither did Narayanrao ask anything, nor did Raghunathrao speak a word. When they reached Raghunathrao's palace, Anandibai was already waiting for them. She started crying when she saw her husband in that condition.

"Narayan, what are you doing to him?" Anandibai questioned Narayanrao, who did not say anything and left with the guards.

"You call him your son and he misses no chance of humiliating you. You have been paraded like a criminal tied in ropes," Anandibai told Raghunathrao who was deeply hurt by the incident and did not say anything.

"I can't take this humiliation anymore, Swari. I can't live with this humiliation..." she cried and dramatically fell at the feet of her husband.

"I also can't tolerate it anymore," responded Raghunathrao and fell on his bed with a thud. He was physically and mentally exhausted.

Raghunathrao, who had been a fierce warrior and was once the right hand of Nanasaheb Peshwa, had been subjected to humiliation many times. This incident had tested his patience. Anandibai wanted to push her husband to the limit so that she could convince him of the sinister plan that she was making. She looked at her husband who was lying on the bed, snoring.

Anandibai was slowly turning the humiliation into a weapon and preparing her husband to avenge the humiliation he had been subjected to after the death of his brother. She convinced him that after the death of Nanasaheb, he had never received his right place in the family.

Anandibai was elated. Her plan was executed with perfection.

It was Narayanrao's turn to react.

THE POONA CONSPIRACY 8

The incident of the night was still heavy on the mind of the Peshwa as he was getting ready for the darbar. It was clear to Narayanrao that his uncle was in constant touch with his supporters and planning a coup. He was so lost in his thoughts that he did not even realize it when Gangabai entered the chamber.

"Are you talking to yourself?" Gangabai interrupted him.

"Sorry, I did not notice you," mumbled Narayanrao.

"I can see that. You seemed lost. What is keeping your mind occupied?" Gangabai asked.

"I am concerned about Kaka's behaviour Ganga. Yesterday night's incident is proof that Kaka is conspiring against me," Narayanrao said in a concerned voice looking away from Gangabai.

"You can have a word with him and other senior ministers about the incident." Gangabai suggested.

"I don't think Kaka would ever change and would ever give up his dream."

"Which dream?" Gangabai had understood what Narayanrao wanted to convey, but still asked a direct question. Narayanrao did not answer her and left for the darbar.

Narayanrao entered the darbar and raised the long-pending succession issue of Nagpur for discussion. He had already gathered more information about the incident of the night.

"Shrimant, the succession issue of Nagpur is a sensitive topic," Ram Shastri sensed the mood of the Peshwa and forewarned him.

"I am aware of that, Shastribuwa," Narayanrao was unfazed by the warning.

"Any decision in that matter should be made with due consideration. We have all the senior ministers here today and it would be good to seek their advice before any decision is being made." Ram Shastri replied and looked at Peshwa who was lost in thoughts. He felt that Narayanrao had not even listened to him and already had something on his mind.

"Shastribuwa, after what happened in Shaniwar Wada last night, I don't think there is any need for a discussion on this subject. We all are aware of the opinion of Dada and what he had suggested before he left us for heavenly abode." Narayanrao tried to assert his opinion on the subject.

"Shrimant Madhavrao had his opinion on this subject, but things have changed since then. I would still advise that we should not make any decision in haste that can put the future of the alliance with Nagpur in danger. In the past also, we have had a difficult relationship with the Bhosles," Ram Shastri spoke freely.

"Raghuji has been adopted by Janoji Bhosle as his legal heir. If we respect his decision then we should go ahead with that arrangement. Janoji wanted Raghuji to be his heir and adoption is the formal procedure for that." Sakharam Bapu shared his thoughts when he was asked.

"The British are expanding in various parts of our motherland. We all know that Mudhoji is a sympathizer of Britishers. That was the reason Shrimant Madhavrao sided with Sabaji who remains a staunch supporter of the empire. I am sure sooner or later

Mudhoji will take the side of the Britishers and may fight a battle against us. As you said Shastribuwa, in the past also we have had a difficult relationship with Nagpur. We should be very careful in what we do now," said Nana Phadnis.

"This is a political decision that can have long-term consequences for the empire. We have to decide at the earliest as the seat can't remain empty for long. Even the British are keenly watching our next steps," Ram Shastri commented.

The discussion in the darbar continued for long and all the ministers shared their opinions with the Peshwa. The Bhosles of Nagpur had a history of a difficult relationship with Marathas. Before joining hands with Madhavrao, Janoji had even fought against the Marathas alongside Nizam. Before breathing his last, Madhavrao had declared his intentions to support the claim of Sabaji to the throne instead of Mudhoji. A formal decision could not be made by Madhavrao, and the issue remained unresolved.

Like many allies of Marathas, Nagpur too had two factions. One was led by Sabaji who had the support of the Peshwa and Nana Phadnis. The other section was led by Mudhoji, a staunch supporter of Raghunathrao. The proceedings of the darbar conveyed that there was no clear consensus on the topic as each side wanted to strengthen their support base across the allies. Narayanrao wanted Sabaji to take charge and Raghunathrao was supporting the claim of Raghuji and Mudhoji.

"We all know what happened yesterday at Shaniwar Wada. It was supported by Mudhoji and his agents here. This shows that Mudhoji has no respect for the Peshwa and he is secretly supporting Kaka to plan a coup against us. This is a clear case of treason against the Peshwa and Mudhoji should be taught a lesson. Today I declare Sabaji Bhosle as the legal heir and the next sena-saheb-subha of Nagpur." After multiple deliberations, Narayanrao announced in the court. It was a decision that was more influenced by the incident of the night than the discussions in the darbar.

"Shrimant, we are going against the wishes of late Janoji Bhosle. He had already declared his legal heir." Sakharam Bapu tried to question the decision announced by Peshwa.

"Bapu, you are speaking against the order of the Peshwa. We have already made a decision and do not need any more consultation on the subject." Narayanrao got angry when Sakharam Bapu tried to intervene in his decision.

"I will make all the necessary arrangements and immediately send a message to Nagpur for the coronation of Sabaji as the sena-saheb-subha of Nagpur. This should take place at the earliest," Nana announced.

"All the agents should immediately leave for Nagpur with the robes of sena-saheb-subha for Sabaji. We will also send Khanderao Darekar with armed reinforcements to support Sabaji to claim the throne if Mudhoji doesn't agree with our order," announced Narayanrao.

There were murmurs in the darbar and the ministers whispered about the sudden announcement. The official order was written and sent to Nagpur along with the robes of sena-saheb-subha. Raghunathrao was upset again with Narayanrao as the Peshwa took a strong stand against the advice of Sakharam Bapu. Ram Shastri and Nana Phadnis were convinced by the decision and supported the Peshwa. Ram Shastri went to the chamber of Narayanrao after the darbar was dispersed.

"Shrimant, I am happy that you have not spoken anything about Dadasaheb in the darbar today. It would have been further humiliation for him." Ram Shastri praised him.

"Shastribuwa, what should I do with Kaka! You suggested allowing him visitors and I did that. Now you have seen what he has done. Kaka tried to escape from captivity and planned to revolt against us. Kaka has not changed in so many years, Shastribuwa."

"Dadasaheb had misused his position and also his freedom, but I still request you to refrain from declaring any harsh punishment for him. It is good that you have not announced any punishment for him in the darbar today. It would have only aggrieved him," Ram Shastri replied.

Ram Shastri was worried about the deteriorating relationship between Peshwa and his uncle. The revolt was not new for Raghunathrao, but Madhavrao had handled the sensitive issue more carefully. The relationship between the two most powerful members of the Peshwa family, who were at loggerheads with each other, was at its lowest point.

Ram Shastri was trying his best to ensure peace between the two as he was aware that it would not be easy to run the affairs of the empire by keeping Raghunathrao at bay.

"I will personally go and meet Kaka soon," Narayanrao replied as Ram Shastri requested him to be careful with his uncle.

"The way Dadasaheb is reacting these days, I feel that all these acts are not planned by him alone. There is someone else who is conspiring. Dadasaheb is always surrounded by people who give him wrong advice and he listens to them."

"Who do you feel could be behind the conspiracy? Mudhoji's agents supported Kaka yesterday, I don't know who else is conspiring against us. We are living in very difficult times, Shastribuwa."

"I am not sure who could be behind Dadasaheb, he has his group of loyalists who could go to any extent to support him. There was a time when he carried the Maratha flag beyond Lahore. Many in the empire respect him for that. Dadasaheb can make alliances and garner support anywhere in the empire and his loyalists will come forward for him. As you have just mentioned, Mudhoji is just one of them." Ram Shastri responded.

Narayanrao thought about the punishment for his uncle. Ram Shastri had advised him to be considerate of his age and position. Narayanrao planned to go and meet him the next day. He was worried about the conversation he would have; it had always been difficult for him to talk to his uncle.

Tuloji reached the chamber of Anandibai with the news. She was eagerly waiting to know the proceedings of the darbar as she was expecting repercussions after the incident. She enthusiastically welcomed Tuloji to her chamber. Anandibai had intentionally skipped the proceedings of the darbar on that day.

"Everything so far has happened as per plan, Tuloji," Anandibai said proudly, Raghunathrao was not there till then and the two of them were talking freely. Tuloji was surprised by the reaction of Anandibai.

"Dadasaheb was captured by the guards and was treated like a criminal again. I still do not understand why you asked me to share Dadasaheb's plan with the guards. If he would ever come to know that I am the one who foiled his plans, he would sever my head in the blink of an eye," a concerned Tuloji said.

"Tuloji, this is part of a bigger plan. It is not easy to go out of Shaniwar Wada, raise a big army, or garner support from allies and attack Poona to snatch the Peshwai. It is impossible to defeat Peshwa in Poona by force. So, even if Swari would have escaped successfully, he would have either got captured or killed in his attempt to overthrow Narayan." Anandibai had keenly observed and meticulously planned the act. She was talking like an experienced war strategist.

"If you knew this then why create all this drama? You could have told this directly to Dadasaheb and that way it would have been easier for everyone." Tuloji questioned.

"I could have, but he would not have listened to me. A man mostly learns from his own mistakes and rarely from his wife."

"This is too confusing for me to understand. What is our plan now?" Tuloji was curious and puzzled.

"Did you manage to meet and have a discussion with Sumer Singh?"

"Yes, I talked to Sumer Singh and he is ready to support us for money. I feel he is a greedy man who is hungry for money and power."

"We all are Tuloji. I was expecting this response from him. Ask Sumer Singh to meet me at the backdoor of my chamber tomorrow evening," Anandibai told Tuloji. She was standing at the entrance of her chamber, appreciating the beauty of the Shaniwar Wada.

Anandibai had not told her specific plan to Tuloji. '*The best-kept secrets are the ones which are with only one person,*' thought Anandibai.

"Dadasaheb, you are not allowed to go out of your chamber!" a guard stopped Raghunathrao at the entrance of his chamber in the morning the next day. He was going out to perform his religious duties which he performed daily under the open sky in broad daylight.

"Who has given this order?" Raghunathrao shouted at the guards.

"We can't say anything, but we were told to guard your chamber and restrict your movement." One of the guards responded.

"Get out of my way immediately or you will be facing my sword." Raghunathrao ordered the guards, but they did not budge from their place.

"There is no need to get angry with the guards, Kaka. I have ordered them to keep a watch on you and not allow you to go out of your chamber," Narayanrao, who was on his way to meet his uncle, replied.

"Narayan, what is this now? You know my daily morning ritual. I pray to the almighty and offer my respects to the Sun god."

"Every part of this world belongs to the almighty, Kaka. You can pray anywhere. As long as our heart and mind are clean, our prayers will be heard by god," Narayanrao said sarcastically.

"What do you want to say Narayan?" asked a puzzled Raghunathrao.

"Let us go inside, Kaka." Narayanrao and Raghunathrao went in.

Raghunathrao was frustrated as he was not allowed to perform his morning ritual. All his religious activities were already curtailed due to shortage of funds. Narayanrao sat inside the chamber with his uncle and Anandibai too joined them.

"Kaka, I thought about yesterday's incident the whole night and discussed it with Shastribuwa also. It was not the first time this has happened; there were multiple incidences when you tried to escape or revolt. You are my uncle and part of the family, but that doesn't mean that you can revolt against the Peshwa. Your act of yesterday is a clear case of treason against the empire," Narayanrao spoke with authority.

"If you want to put me in jail or torture me to death, please do that Narayan, but don't humiliate me again and again," Raghunathrao responded with no remorse on his face.

Anandibai was keenly listening to the discussion between the two. The discussion between the two members of the Peshwa family was happening as per her expectations.

"Kaka, I don't want to put you in jail. You will remain in your chamber, but for some time you won't be allowed to go out. Kakubai will have no such restrictions." Narayanrao decided to be considerate to his uncle and aunt. Anandibai felt relieved that she had been given the freedom to venture out of her chamber without any restrictions.

"Narayan, I can't live like this in captivity forever. I want to retire and go on a pilgrimage." Raghunathrao almost pleaded to Narayanrao, but he did not budge from his decision and left. He had nothing more to discuss with his uncle.

"I told you this earlier also, no one cares for you. Now Narayanrao has also started treating you like a criminal." Anandibai was talking to her husband after Narayanrao had left their chamber.

"I need to speak to Bapu about this. This can't go forever. Last time I ended my hunger strike, but this time I will sit on hunger strike and will not end till I get absolute freedom. I have tolerated humiliation at the hands of Madhav for years; I won't tolerate this again." Raghunathrao was burning with rage, his voice was quivering and his hands were trembling.

"You don't earn the freedom by protests, strikes, or by leaving your food. You are not a weak person who should beg for his freedom. This is the time for the warrior in you to wake up and fight for your right," Anandibai said dramatically.

"What do you mean by that? Do you want me to fight a war with Narayan? I have already fought with Madhav and lost my prestige in that battle."

"That was a bad idea, to fight the Peshwa for the throne and this time also, I won't suggest you do that. It is good that your escape plan was foiled. Fighting Narayan from outside the Shaniwar Wada would be futile." Anandibai was slowly revealing her plans.

"In that case, I have to live my whole life like a prisoner of the Peshwa," Raghunathrao said in a sad voice. It was at this moment that servant announced the arrival of Tuloji. Anandibai instructed the servant to send him in.

"All your life you have fought for this empire and won so many battles and earned revenue for the royal treasury. When Nanasaheb died, it was you who should have been made the Peshwa, but you were ignored and Madhav was given Peshwai. Madhav was a child then. No one cared about your devotion. You are also the son of the great Bajirao Peshwa and had all the rights to become the Peshwa after your brother. If your brother can get the Peshwai, why not you Swari?" Anandibai questioned her husband.

"You are right. Dadasaheb was always ignored like a stepson. He had commanded all the respect in the Maratha empire, but never got his due from the family." Tuloji further added fuel to the fire.

"When Madhav died, you were again ignored and Narayan, who had no understanding of running the affairs of an empire, was made the Peshwa. That was your last chance to become the Peshwa and that has also passed. I think you are right, Swari. We have to live as prisoners of the Peshwa for the rest of our lives," Anandibai said philosophically.

Raghunathrao was patiently listening to the conversation, but did not say anything. Tuloji looked towards Anandibai; she instructed him to continue.

"There is still time, Dadasaheb," Tuloji said cunningly.

"Yes, there is time. But Swari won't agree to the plan." Anandibai responded even before Raghunathrao could speak.

"Dadasaheb, you have seen everything unfolding in front of your eyes. Today your movement is restricted, tomorrow you might be put in jail, your religious activities, your finances, and even your food would be restricted someday," Tuloji continued.

"The son of great Bajirao Peshwa would die the death of a prisoner at the hands of his nephew!" Anandibai commented.

She was testing his patience before putting forward her plan and convincing him to be a part of it. She was aware of the behaviour of her husband and his affection for the family. It had happened earlier with Madhavrao at Alegaon. It was his love for his nephew that stopped him from taking the power. Anandibai did not want the repeat of the same mistake. Her plan had to be executed with perfection.

"I can't let this continue forever. Tuloji, for how long Swari will tolerate this humiliation?" Anandibai asked a question seeing her husband had not responded, but was keenly listening to the conversation.

"There is a way out, Dadasaheb. We can't fight Narayanrao by leaving Shaniwar Wada, but we can fight Narayanrao while being inside the Shaniwar Wada." Tuloji gave a hint about the plan to Raghunathrao.

Raghunathrao listened to both of them and in the end, Anandibai exerted her influence over her husband, who agreed to her plan.

Later in the evening, the backdoor of Raghunathrao's chamber was not lit and the guards had been removed from the duty. Sumer Singh was standing there along with Khadak Singh. Both of them were waiting for the arrival of Anandibai.

The backdoor of the chamber slowly opened. Anandibai was careful. She checked in all the directions and came out of the chamber. Sumer Singh and Khadak Singh, both wished her. Anandibai responded back.

She handed Sumer Singh a piece of paper that had the official order written on it with the seal of Raghunathrao. Khadak Singh rushed to get the flambeau and then Sumer Singh opened the paper to read it. His eyes widened with shock by the time he finished reading it.

"But this is not what I had discussed earlier!" Sumer Singh responded. He was stunned by the order he had just received.

"This is your new order Sumer Singh," Anandibai said calmly.

Sumer Singh read the order again. It took him a while to understand the seriousness of the order and the risks involved in executing it.

"Sarkar, I will ensure that order is executed, but our earlier deal stands cancelled," Sumer Singh told Anandibai.

They talked for some time. Then Sumer Singh put forward his demands to execute the order and Anandibai agreed to all his demands.

"You will be given whatever you ask for!" Anandibai told Sumer Singh.

"I will execute the order." Sumer Singh confirmed.

Sumer Singh and Khadak Singh saluted Anandibai, who responded with an evil grin on her face.

9 THE JUDGEMENT DAY

October 1773
Maratha Darbar, Alegaon

The Maratha darbar had gathered for the coronation of Raghunathrao and would be Peshwa was not expecting the sudden turn of events. Ram Shastri had a reputation across the empire. So, when he declared in the darbar that he had completed his investigation into the murder of Narayanrao Peshwa and was ready to announce the judgement, everyone was spellbound. Those present in the darbar were so stunned by the announcement that everyone was looking towards Ram Shastri. There was absolute silence, and no one was even whispering. It was clear to all those present that Ram Shastri was up to something.

Ram Shastri, who already had the judgement on his mind, decided not to reveal the results of his investigation to the darbar directly. It would not be easy for him to announce the judgement and execute it. Along with the announcement of the judgement, he intended to garner the support from the darbar to stand against evil.

The Chief Justice of the Maratha empire, who had the duty to take the new Peshwa to the throne, was standing between the throne and the new Peshwa. The fearless Ram Shastri had halted the proceedings of the coronation of Raghunathrao and he had chosen this particular occasion to deliver the judgement on the murder of Narayanrao Peshwa.

"Dadasaheb! This is the seat of Marathas. On this seat, Shrimant Bajirao sat in the past. With his courage and bravery, he not only expanded the Maratha empire, but also defeated many enemies. Shrimant Nanasaheb, while being on this seat took the flag of Marathas to Attock. When Shrimant Madhavrao sat on this seat, he recaptured Delhi in the north and defeated Haider and Nizam Ali in the south. When Shrimant Madhavrao died, do you remember what you promised to him?" Ram Shastri asked Raghunathrao.

"Yes Shastribuwa, I do remember," Raghunathrao struggled with words.

The arrival of Ram Shastri had made him happy, but the sudden announcement about the judgement on trial into the murder of Narayanrao Peshwa had made Raghunathrao nervous.

"I also remember what I had promised to Shrimant Madhavrao on his death bed. I could not keep my promise, Dadasaheb. I will regret for the rest of my life that I could not keep the words I gave to Shrimant Madhavrao. Could you keep your promise to Shrimant Madhavrao?" Ram Shastri sensed the nervousness on Raghunathrao's face and questioned him again in a loud voice with a clear intention that everyone present in the darbar should hear his words.

"What do you mean, Shastribuwa?" Raghunathrao was quaking by the questioning in an open darbar. He was finding it difficult to control his emotions, his frustration was reflecting on his face. *'I made a mistake by inviting Ram Shastri for the coronation ceremony,'* thought Raghunathrao. But it was too late.

The dignitaries present in the court were getting edgy. Most of them were aware of the happenings of the last few months, but the political equations in the empire were such at that time that no one wanted to go against the wishes of Raghunathrao, who himself had taken over the power and was now going to take the Peshwai. The support for Raghunathrao was mainly for two reasons. The first was that Raghunathrao had his group of sympathizers among many generals of Marathas and commanded respect across the allies. The second reason was more delicate. The Peshwa family had no male heir at that time other than Raghunathrao. If he would not be appointed the next Peshwa, it could lead to a big political crisis, ultimately resulting in the collapse of the empire. Many enemies were closely observing the happenings of Poona and any wrong step at such times could lead to a political crisis for Marathas.

"I would tell you in detail, Dadasaheb. You promised Shrimant Madhavrao that you would protect Shrimant Narayanrao as your son. You said that nothing would happen to him till you are alive. What happened to your promise? Shrimant Narayanrao is no more with us." Ram Shastri reiterated the fact about the murder of Narayanrao, his face red with anger and his voice louder than normal.

"I could not keep my promise, Shastribuwa. It is so unfortunate that Narayanrao died, and I am standing here alive to take his place. My Narayan is no more, Shastribuwa," Raghunathrao said dramatically.

Anandibai was intently listening to the conversation. She was already frustrated by the sudden arrival of Ram Shastri and the delay had further irked her. She controlled herself to maintain the dignity of the darbar and did not speak against the judge, but when the questioning continued, she could not hold herself.

"What is going on, Shastribuwa? Swari has waited for you for so long and the ceremony is already delayed due to your late arrival. Why are you delaying it further?" Anandibai was getting anxious and she questioned Ram Shastri. Gardis were ready in their positions.

"Dadasaheb, go ahead and claim the throne. Sit on the musnud. Vahinisaheb is getting impatient. Your dream of becoming Peshwa will be fulfilled. History would remember you as the Peshwa of Marathas. Your name would go down in the golden history of the Maratha empire. But remember one thing, Dadasaheb, the future generations will ask about the gruesome murders at Shaniwar Wada." Ram Shastri retorted without even looking towards Anandibai.

"Shastribuwa, why are you playing with words? Why don't you tell everyone what you have on your mind?" Anandibai questioned Ram Shastri again. Raghunathrao did not intervene in their conversation.

She was confident that Ram Shastri would not make any statement against Ragnunathrao in a full darbar. Anandibai had made all the arrangements to avoid any revolt or coup against her husband and that was the reason the coronation was happening in Alegaon, far away from Poona. She had no idea what Ram Shastri had done in the last few weeks and what he had uncovered in his investigation.

"Vahinisaheb, you want to know what is there on my mind? As the Chief Justice of Marathas, my mind is concerned about the future of the empire. My mind is concerned about this seat which had been occupied by visionary leaders who always thought about their subjects. This seat which was always the pride of Hindustan deserves the finest leaders who will always keep the interests of the empire before their own. Those who would protect the good and fight the evil. Those who would carry forward the legacy of Chhatrapati Shivaji Maharaj!" Ram Shastri turned towards Anandibai and spoke to the whole darbar with open hands.

"You are right, Shastribuwa. This seat would be honoured to have one more visionary leader today," Anandibai spoke for her husband with a cunning smile on her face.

Ram Shastri stared at Anandibai, who was sitting on the upper floor of the darbar, reserved for women members of the empire. Anandibai was intentionally looking in the other direction. Ram Shastri waited for a few moments, but Anandibai did not look at him. He turned back towards Raghunathrao as he had some more questions for him.

"Dadasaheb, before you take this seat, I request you to explain the incidents of that fateful day to the darbar," Ram Shastri said, the request seemed like an order from the judge.

Those present in the darbar had heard about the incidents that had taken place that day. Most of them had heard different versions of it, depending on from whom they were hearing and to which side they belonged. The ones who had sympathy for Narayanrao had heard a very different version of the incident. The supporters of Raghunathrao had heard another version of the incident. There were many rumours also which further added to the confusion. There were only a few people who knew exactly what had transpired inside Shaniwar Wada that day.

"I don't remember clearly. There were riots inside the palace on that day and there was chaos everywhere. Gardis were angry with Narayan as their salaries were not paid and they had created a ruckus. In that chaos and riots, we lost our Narayan," Raghunathrao spoke in a broken voice.

"Why were there riots inside the palace on that day?" Ram Shastri asked Raghunathrao, calmed down by now.

"I have already told this, Shastribuwa. Gardis had financial issues pending for long and their salaries were not paid. To protest against that, they were creating ruckus inside the palace on that day. They had done that earlier also and Narayan was aware of their problems," Raghunathrao replied in a low voice that was hardly audible. He was still not looking towards Ram Shastri.

"I know that Gardis had financial issues and their salaries were delayed. They are the official guards of Shaniwar Wada. They gathered so much courage to create a ruckus inside the capital palace of Marathas and attack the Peshwa in those riots! This is difficult to believe, Dadasaheb. Where were you on that day?" Ram Shastri continued the questioning.

"I was inside my chamber, Shastribuwa. My guards came rushing to me and told me that Gardis are creating a ruckus and asked me not to go out. I decided to stay inside my chamber only as there was no clarity on what was happening outside."

"Your guards warned you about the danger, but did they tell you anything about the danger to other family members? Did you think about the safety of Shrimant Narayanrao? Did you go out to help him? Did Shrimant come to your chamber to ask you for help?" Ram Shastri was pinning him down with his questions.

Ram Shastri was aware of the events of that day with all the minute details. He wanted to recreate the crime scene for the darbar to highlight the seriousness of the heinious crime that was committed on that day inside Shaniwar Wada.

"Shastribuwa, Swari has already told you that it was in riots that Narayan died. Why are you asking the same question again and again?" Anandibai felt that her husband was on trial. She questioned the stand of Ram Shastri as Raghunathrao was not confronting him.

"Dadasaheb, I am asking you. Did Shrimant come to your chamber to ask for help?" Ram Shastri again repeated his question. He spoke so loudly that even the guards standing at the entrance turned their heads to listen.

The continuous questioning in the full darbar had its impact on Raghunathrao and he could no longer tolerate the barbs from Ram Shastri. Raghunathrao got emotional at the moment and burst out.

"I have not killed Narayan, Shastribuwa. I have not killed Narayan..." Raghunathrao was almost crying in full darbar, but Ram Shastri was firm at his place.

"Then tell the darbar who killed Shrimant Narayanrao. Tell the truth of that fateful day. As the judge of the empire, I order you to tell everyone what happened on that day inside Shaniwar Wada." Ram Shastri ordered with a glowering face.

The atmosphere of the darbar had completely changed after the arrival of Ram Shastri and his questioning of the would be Peshwa. The dignitaries present in the darbar also felt that they were not witnessing a coronation ceremony anymore.

They were witnessing a trial in the court of Ram Shastri Prabhune.

SHANIWAR WADA UNDER SIEGE 10

The evening of 30th August 1773
Shaniwar Wada, Poona

Those who had arrived at Shaniwar Wada since afternoon were not allowed to enter and all the gates remained closed. Slowly a crowd started gathering at all the gates of Shaniwar Wada and the news spread in the city. Nana Phadnis was at his house when the news reached him. At first, he did not believe it as the capital palace of Marathas housed the Peshwa family and was the most secured place in the empire. There had been many rumours floating around in Poona and he too considered it to be a rumour, but he decided to check himself nonetheless. Nana immediately left his house for Shaniwar Wada.

It was shocking and inconceivable for everyone in Poona city. The palace which housed the Peshwa family had been under siege and was completely disconnected from the external world.

'If the news would prove to be true, and spread to other parts of the empire, it would send a wrong message across the empire which was already in turmoil due to the family dispute,' thought Nana on his way.

There had been no news of what had transpired inside the Shaniwar Wada or what was happening. The movement was restricted since afternoon, and no one was allowed to enter or leave the premises. There had been no communication from inside. All the gates of the palace remained close since then. Ganeshotsav celebrations were going on and many senior ministers were not on duty, which further led to the confusion and chaos.

Haripant Phadke was the last person who had met Peshwa in the afternoon and then left the palace. Everything seemed normal to him at that time. He had come to his house for lunch and was resting after lunch when a guard came rushing to his house.

"Sarkar, Gardis have closed all the gates of Shaniwar Wada and are not allowing anyone to enter or leave," blurted out the guard.

"What are you saying? When did this happen? Are you sure?" Haripant was startled to hear the news and questioned the guard.

"This has happened in the afternoon and since then all the gates are closed. Not even Gardis are allowed to enter or leave. There has been no movement at any of the gates of the palace." The guard responded.

"Any idea what could have happened?" Haripant asked, aware of the fact that the guard might not have any clue about the incident.

"There are rumours that Gardis have created riots inside to protest against their salaries."

"You go and inform Nana Phadnis about this. Tell him, I want him to come and meet me at the palace immediately." Haripant dispatched the guard to the house of Nana Phadnis and rushed to Shaniwar Wada. Nana had already left his house.

On his way, Haripant was thinking about the discussion he had had in the morning with Narayanrao. '*Can Gardis dare to siege Shaniwar Wada on their own, just for their salaries?*' thought Haripant and the answer to the question seemed no to him. There had been minor issues earlier also by the Gardis, but putting the palace under seige for the salaries was unprecedented. The absolute closure of the gates and no communication from inside were intimidating. '*Have the guards taken the Peshwa family as their hostage?*' Haripant wondered.

When Haripant reached Shaniwar Wada, he saw that some soldiers from his troops had already gathered at Dilli Darwaza. He had a word with them, but no one had any clue.

Haripant surveyed the palace from outside. He was puzzled by the seizure of the palace. It was a little late in the afternoon, but the sun was still up in the sky and there was sufficient light to survey all the posts around the palace. Haripant stood near the wall of the palace to hear some noises from inside. There were sounds of people moving inside; he could hear the wailing sound of women and men crying with pain, but could not decipher much from that. It was impossible to guess what was going on inside and his heart was sinking with a feeling that something sinister had happened. He went around the palace and finally stopped in front of the Ganesh Darwaza.

"I order you to open the gates!" Haripant shouted at the gate as he could not see anyone. He was not even sure if anyone was there behind the gates.

"We are ordered not to open the gates for anyone." The response from the other side of the gate was shocking for him.

"Who are you and who gave you that order?" Haripant asked authoritatively.

He had his sword in his hand and some of his armed soldiers were standing behind him. Haripant was aware that it would not be easy to force open the doors of the palace with his troops.

"We can't tell you anything, but the gates can't be opened at this time." The guard responded.

"Open the gates now or I will kill you!" Haripant shouted at the guards. He was getting tense as the suspense was getting on his nerves. After all, the palace housed the most powerful family of the empire.

"Don't try to create a scene here. We are just following orders. The orders are to keep everyone out. We will follow our orders till our death." The guards said in unison.

It was not a response he was expecting from the guards. Haripant moved away from the gate and remembered his conversation with Narayanrao in the morning. Narayanrao had informed him about the threat to his life. Now, this siege of Shaniwar Wada and such behaviour of the guards had spooked him.

Haripant immediately sent a message and planned the gathering of his troops. He was concerned about the coup. This was the first time in Maratha history that the palace had been completely disconnected from the outside world. He was concerned about the safety of Narayanrao and others inside. Haripant knew that it would take some time for the troops to gather for any armed action against the guards and to breach the gates of the palace. But if they delayed it, the situation could only get worse. Under such a situation, quick action was always more beneficial than the right action.

"What is going on Haripant?" Nana asked him when he arrived.

"The guards have closed all the access to the palace. They are not allowing anyone to go inside or come out. There is no message from anyone, absolutely no communication with anyone inside."

"Did you try to send any message to Shrimant or Dadasaheb?" Nana asked.

"No, I did not." Haripant responded.

Haripant was focused on the opening of the gate and had not tried to talk to the guard to communicate with Narayanrao or Raghunathrao. As time passed, tension outside the Shaniwar Wada grew. No one was aware of what had happened inside the Maratha Palace.

"It seems the Gardis had taken everyone hostage." Haripant told Nana.

Nana Phadnis thought for a while and when he saw Gardis protecting every gate and wall of Shaniwar Wada, he feared the worst. Nana was hearing the rumours about the coup for weeks, but he had ignored those rumours. Such rumours were not uncommon in the empire at that time.

"We have to go inside somehow," Nana said, realizing that in such a situation, time is very precious.

"The guards are protecting every gate of the palace. Every entry point to the palace is sealed. I am sure Gardis are certainly involved in whatever is happening. Only they know Shaniwar Wada so well that they can seal it so quickly without arising any suspicion," replied Haripant.

Nana looked around the palace for a while and decided to strike a conversation with the Gardis.

"I know that you won't allow us to enter the palace, but can you tell me who has ordered the closure of all the gates?" Nana tried to gather some information from the Gardis at Ganesh Darwaza.

"We have no information to share with anyone. We are told to keep the gates closed till further orders." A guard responded back.

"Can I talk to Sumer Singh?" Nana Phadnis requested.

"We have instructions to not take any requests for meeting anyone." The guard was now getting irritated by the questions. Nana realized that the discussion would not yield desirable results.

"Can you pass my message to Shrimant or Dadasaheb that Nana Phadnis is outside and wants to meet them immediately?" Nana requested the guard, who reluctantly took the message.

The message was passed to another guard, who went inside. Nana Phadnis was not sure if the message would even be delivered and if there would be any response. He did not want to waste any time waiting for the response and decided to go and meet Ram Shastri.

"Haripant, gather your troops as early as possible. It is going to be a very long and dark night." Nana told Haripant. Nana wanted to take no chance and was preparing even for an armed action.

Nana too walked around the periphery of Shaniwar Wada. It was strange that every nook and corner of the palace was heavily protected from any possible intrusion from inside. There was no possibility of breaching the Gardis. He too tried to stand closer to the palace walls to hear some noise from inside, but there was very little that he could hear. Some children were still sobbing inside, and the wailing sound of women, worried him a bit.

There was a sinister silence around the walls of the Shaniwar-Wada. The capital palace of the Maratha empire was under siege.

"Good that you came! I was thinking of coming and meeting you, Nana." Ram Shastri welcomed Nana Phadnis at his home.

"I have come to inform you about the situation at the palace." Nana told him.

"I have heard some rumours, but not sure what is true and what is not. Are you coming from the palace?"Ram Shastri asked him.

"Yes, Shastribuwa. Unfortunately, the situation is not good. Gardis have closed all the gates and are not allowing any movement in and out of the palace. Whatever we know till now is based on rumours only. I doubt anyone outside Shaniwar Wada is aware of what exactly has happened inside. There is no communication with people inside. I have tried to send a message to Shrimant and Dadasaheb, but I am not sure whether it will be delivered or not."

"This is a very strange situation. Shrimant and Dadasaheb both are inside the palace. What do you think would have happened?" a concerned Ram Shastri asked.

"It is difficult to say what would have happened inside. The way Gardis are protecting the palace, I feel whatever had happened, Gardis are at the center of it. They were not happy for a few months, but I doubt that they would take such an extreme step of seizing the palace for their salaries. They know the consequences of such an act. This is something beyond their salaries, this is something beyond Gardis..." Nana said thoughtfully.

"I also feel so, this is not about Gardis and their salaries. This is certainly something else." Ram Shastri agreed with Nana.

Nana had inklings of what could have happened inside the palace. The way the family dispute had played out inside the palace since the death of Madhavrao, Nana was certain that his hunch was right.

"We have learned from history how power shifts in the Mughal empire. I am now worried if Marathas are going to do the same." Nana shared his fears with Ram Shastri.

"Do you mean Dadasaheb could be behind all this?" Ram Shastri understood what Nana wanted to convey. Every living being in the Maratha empire was aware of Raghunathrao's ambitions.

"Dadasaheb has always been close to Mughals and had learned a lot from their culture and values. He had revolted in the past also at Alegaon and no wonder he could attempt something similar again," Nana replied.

"We need quick access to Shaniwar Wada in that case. Talking to Dadasaheb could help ease our case. He gets carried away by his emotions, but it is not difficult to convince him with logic. Any delay would only create more problems. We should talk to Bapu." Ram Shastri suggested as Sakharam Bapu was close to Raghunathrao.

"I am worried that logic may not work now. I see a long battle ahead for us. This could be the beginning of a civil war, Shastribuwa," Nana said in a concerned voice.

"You go to the palace and try to get in touch with Shrimant or Dadasaheb. I am worried about the safety of everyone inside. I will go and meet Bapu. If Dadasaheb has planned something, Bapu might know about it." Ram Shastri comforted Nana.

Nana Phadnis left for Shaniwar Wada. By the time he reached, Haripant had gathered a troop of more than two thousand armed soldiers who had surrounded the palace from outside. Trimbakrao had also arrived by then, but there was no sign of any message from inside.

"I think we should make a decision as early as possible. Any delay could create more chaos and more tension only." Trimbakrao told Nana.

"Haripant, which are the points from where we can forcefully enter the palace? There would be some weak points from where we can break in?" Nana asked Haripant Phadke.

The irony was that the protectors of Shaniwar Wada were searching the ways to attack it. Haripant Phadke had knowledge of every part of Shaniwar Wada as he had been part of the Maratha empire and security of the Peshwa for a long period. He was aware of the weakness of the palace also.

"Confrontation could put us in a difficult situation. We can climb the walls near Dilli Darwaza during the night. The other option is to use the water supply line to enter the palace, but that is very risky." Haripant suggested. It was at this moment that Ram Shastri also joined them.

"Shrimant Narayanrao and Gangabai are inside the palace and we can't risk their lives by forcefully entering it. If Gardis sense our plan, they could harm Shrimant," Ram Shastri told them.

They discussed for a while and could not agree on any plan. There was still some time for the sunset. The daylight was slowly fading away and guards had not lighted the lamps around the palace. The troops were ready and waiting for the order. Suddenly they saw the small gate at Ganesh Darwaza open and a guard came towards them.

"Dadasaheb wants to meet Nana Phadnis and Trimbakrao. Only two of them are allowed to come inside. No weapons are allowed." The guard declared.

"They are senior ministers of the empire. They will carry their weapons and I will also join them." Haripant protested with his sword in his hand.

"Haripant, let us follow as they say. Nana and Trimbakrao can handle this." Ram Shastri commented.

"As this is the message from Dadasaheb, I am sure he is behind all this drama. Haripant, keep your troops ready for any action. If you see any movement near the outer periphery of the palace, you must stop it. No one should be allowed to go out of the palace without my permission." Nana gave instructions to Haripant.

"I am worried now, Nana. Make sure that you do not come back without meeting Shrimant and having a clear word with him, even if Dadasaheb resists the meeting," said Ram Shastri.

"Yes, Shastribuwa. We will meet Shrimant and won't come back without meeting him," Nana confirmed.

Sakharam Bapu had also arrived at Ganesh Darwaza as Ram Shastri could not meet him at his house. Nana and Haripant asked the guard to wait as they wanted to have a word with Sakharam Bapu to check if he was aware of any plans of Raghunathrao.

"Bapu, any idea what could have happened inside the Shaniwar Wada?" Ram Shastri asked.

"I don't know, but Dadasaheb had interacted with Nagpur agents many times in the last few days and I sensed that they were up to something," replied Sakharam Bapu.

"That was to plan the escape only or was there some other plan behind the meeting?" asked Nana.

"All I know was that when I last met Dadasaheb a few days back, he was very upset with his continuous house arrest and was desperate for freedom." Sakharam told the truth. There was no new information, so Nana signalled the guard to take them inside.

The guard escorted them through the Ganesh Darwaza. Both of them followed the guard to enter the palace.

They had never seen Shaniwar Wada like that ever before; things were scattered across the palace. Broken utensils were lying everywhere, clothes lay scattered. Some pillars had been damaged and the ceiling had broken. There was dust on the floor and it seemed the whole palace was damaged in a sand storm. Some guards were cleaning the steps when they walked up and Nana could see the red-coloured water flowing down the steps. The sounds of children sobbing, women wailing and men crying with pain only got louder as they walked inside, but they could not see anyone. They were going through a corridor that was kept dark.

Raghunathrao was standing at the entrance of his chamber, expressionless. Nana looked at him and realized that Raghunathrao was waiting for them; he looked pale and defeated. Nana looked at Raghunathrao's hand. It was covered with a cloth and had a red spot in the middle of it showing that he had recently got a wound.

Nana and Trimbakrao wished Raghunathrao and he responded meekly, with a heavy heart as he entered his chamber and both of them followed him.

Nana and Trimbakrao were stunned when they saw the scene inside Raghunathrao's chamber.

Nana's worst fears had come true.

11 THE JUDGEMENT DAY

October 1773
Maratha Darbar, Alegaon

There was absolute silence in the darbar. Ram Shastri had a reputation of being an honest judge with the highest integrity. When he was questioning the would-be Peshwa, all the people present in the darbar were listening to him spellbound.

Anandibai, who was already frustrated with the delay in the coronation ceremony, feared what if Ram Shastri knew the truth. She had covered everything to ensure that no one ever got to know anything about the conspiracy. She had her hands clasped and was constantly tapping her fingers on the other hand due to nervousness.

'Does Ram Shastri *know about the incident of that day?'* her heart was sinking.

"Shastribuwa, if you already know the truth, you can tell the darbar. Everyone present here is eager to know the truth from you," Mahadji Scindia requested Ram Shastri.

The Maratha empire had been in crisis for over a year. The unexpected illness of Madhavrao Peshwa and his untimely death had left the empire in shock and grief. The empire was still recovering from the death of Madhavrao Peshwa when it got another jolt in the form of the conspiracy at Shaniwar Wada. The murder of Narayanrao Peshwa was the most heinous crime that Marathas had ever witnessed. Political confinements, trials, and executions for the sake of power were a common practice in the Mughal empire, but Marathas had never witnessed that.

This murder had set a wrong and immoral precedence.

Ram Shastri was abreast of the fact that the murder of a family member for the sake of power was not the way Marathas work. The event had disgraced the empire. He wanted to make sure that the culprit was punished and that a strong message should be sent across the political spectrum. It was the legacy of Shivaji Maharaj that was at stake and Ram Shastri knew the cost that the Maratha empire would have to pay to safeguard its values.

"I am also equally eager to share the truth with all the dignitaries present here. All Maratha allies, loyalists, ministers, and the public have the right to know the truth. The truth, which is about the murder of their leader, the truth, which is about the breach of trust which Shrimant had, the truth about the conspiracies that were hatched behind closed doors inside Shaniwar Wada, and the truth which is about the greed for power. Truth is supreme and it can be hidden or suppressed, but it cannot be changed.' Ram Shastri spoke in a loud and clear voice.

"We all are eager to know the truth, Shastribuwa. You have always been the epitome of justice for the Marathas. We request you to speak your heart out to the darbar," Mahadji Scindia again requested Ram Shastri.

Ram Shastri nodded and acknowledged the request made by Mahadji Scindia. He could have told the truth at the beginning itself, but just telling the truth on his own was not his intent.

Ram Shastri wanted Raghunathrao to speak the truth in the darbar.

"It would be good if Dadasaheb himself would tell this court what had happened on that day inside Shaniwar Wada. Dadasaheb was present inside the palace at the time of the incident. It would be wise to hear the truth from his mouth." Ram Shastri turned to Raghunathrao who was standing with his head hung low, just a few steps away from the seat of the Maratha empire.

"Dadasaheb?" Ram Shastri looked towards Raghunathrao with eyes wide open, raised eyebrows, and open hands raised in the air signalling to him that it was an order. It was a difficult situation for Raghunathrao to stay silent any longer. Ram Shastri would not let him go without speaking the truth. He was in a dilemma.

Silence would not confirm his innocence. It would do exactly the opposite.

"Shastribuwa, on that day there was chaos created by Gardis inside Shaniwar Wada, and in those riots that tragic incident happened. We lost Narayan," Raghunathrao said meekly.

"You have already told that, Dadasaheb. Let me repeat my question. When Gardis were creating ruckus inside Shaniwar Wada, did Shrimant Narayanrao come to you asking for help?" Ram Shastri asked.

"Yes, Narayan did come to me for help." Raghunathrao told the truth finally, hearing which, there were murmurs in the darbar.

Anandibai twitched in her seat, sweating profusely. It was clear to her by then that Ram Shastri had uncovered something concrete during his investigation. A person of his stature and intelligence would not challenge the Peshwa in the darbar without any concrete proof.

"That is quite natural for Shrimant to come to you for help. You were the eldest member of the Peshwa family in the palace so he thought that you would be the most suited person to help him. So, did you help him? Did you protect Shrimant during the rioting?" Ram Shastri asked the most difficult question.

"Yes, I did. I protected Narayanrao from Gardis who were running behind him," Raghunathrao responded. His reputation and his valour were at stake. The Maratha warrior who had been the right hand of Shrimant Nanasaheb and had carried the Maratha flag beyond Lahore was finding it difficult to speak in the darbar.

"I am not the only one who respects your courage and valour, Dadasaheb. All the dignitaries present in the darbar today and many other Maratha loyalists respect you for your bravery. When I think about the incident of that day, I could not get the answer to a question. Dadasaheb was inside Shaniwar Wada, how could Gardis gather so much courage to create a ruckus in his presence? Dadasaheb, how could Gardis muster so much courage??" Ram Shastri questioned Raghunathrao.

"I don't know, Shastribuwa." Raghunathrao had nothing else to say.

It was ironic that the man who was about to become the Peshwa was standing with his head hung low in a full darbar in front of all the dignitaries.

"You don't know or you don't want to tell?" Ram Shastri questioned him again. Anandibai was furious at the sudden turn of events. Sumer Singh was also at unease by then. He had been the in-charge of security for the ceremony and had sufficient troops deployed inside and around the venue.

"Dadasaheb, it is okay if you are so ashamed about the happenings of that day that you can't even speak about it. We all know the battles you have fought for the empire. Nanasaheb had always respected your courage and bravery. It was you who carried the flag of Marathas beyond Lahore. Today, if he would have been alive, he too would have been ashamed of the event that transpired inside Shaniwar Wada. Guilt about your sins is a natural feeling." Ram Shastri said this looking towards all the dignitaries. Everyone looked at him as he started peeling the layers of his investigation.

"Ram Shastri!" Sumer Singh shouted and raised his sword.

Ram Shastri looked towards Sumer Singh, who was ready to charge at him. He could not believe his own eyes; he smiled at Sumer Singh. Before Sumer Singh could move closer to Ram Shastri, he was stopped by Mahadji.

"Shastribuwa, for the benefit of all present here, I request you to speak the truth," Mahadji implored again.

"Dadasaheb, you said you protected Shrimant from Gardis, but we lost Shrimant on that day. If you were protecting him, how did we lose him?" Ram Shastri's method of revealing the truth was working.

"No, Shastribuwa... I could not save my Narayan..." Raghunathrao said in a sad voice.

"Shrimant Narayanrao trusted Dadasaheb and ran to him for help, but Dadasaheb is saying that he could not protect him from Gardis. This seat of Marathas would be disgraced if a person who could not even protect the Peshwa from the attackers sits on it today." Ram Shastri made a statement that stunned everyone in the court.

"Ram Shastri, mind your words when you speak about Shrimant Raghunathrao Peshwa." Sumer Singh took out his sword again and charged at him.

"This is not the Mughal darbar, Sumer Singh. This is the court of Marathas. Here power can't be snatched away by brandishing your sword." Ram Shastri responded.

He was expecting this from Sumer Singh, but he remained firm at his place to face him. He had nothing to protect himself, but the truth. The dignitaries were observing the unexpected proceedings of the darbar with awe.

"Stop, Sumer Singh!" Mahadji Scindia also took out his sword and ordered Sumer Singh to stop. The latter receded his steps.

"Shastribuwa, for the honour of this seat, we had fought many battles and made many sacrifices. We have served this seat for a long time and have huge respect for this seat. By making such a statement in front of all the dignitaries present here, you are insulting this great seat of Marathas along with all the loyalists who fought for it," Mahadji said to Ram Shastri .

"I understand the sacrifices made by all the Marathas and their allies. That is the very reason I made that statement. My intention is not to insult anyone. I intend to protect this seat and its honour as you have always done. You have done that by your sword. I am doing that by performing my duty as the judge," Ram Shastri replied.

"Then why are you making such statements? What is the meaning of these statements, Shastribuwa? Dadasaheb gave you respect and declared that you would continue to be the Chief Justice. He should be respected the same way as his predecessors." Mahadji questioned the stand of Ram Shastri.

"Dadasaheb, you tried to protect Shrimant, but still, we lost him, which means you were near him when he was killed. I understand that you could not protect him and he was killed in your presence. I request you to tell the court who killed Shrimant Narayanrao?" Ram Shastri finally came to the main point in his investigation.

"Gardis killed Narayan," Raghunathrao spoke the truth again, he had no option.

"Shrimant was killed in your chamber in front of your eyes, and you remained a mute spectator?"Ram Shastri commented, but Raghunathrao had nothing to say.

"Now that you have admitted that Gardis killed Shrimant, can you tell the name of the Gardis who killed him?" This question put Raghunathrao in a difficult spot.

Anandibai looked towards Sumer Singh. The coronation ceremony had taken a completely different turn, which she was not expecting. Raghunathrao was still standing with his head hung low.

"Dadasaheb, can you please tell the darbar the name of the Gardis who killed Shrimant Narayanrao Peshwa?" Ram Shastri said in a loud voice so that everyone present in the darbar could hear the question.

Raghunathrao knew he had no choice, but to answer the question. He had already admitted that he had witnessed the crime.

Raghunathrao finally raised his head and looked towards Ram Shastri, who was looking back at him. Raghunathrao meekly whispered the names of the Gardis who were behind the murder of the Peshwa.

"I could not hear, Dadasaheb. Can you please face the darbar and speak loudly so that I and everyone else present in the darbar can hear?" Ram Shastri ordered.

Raghunathrao turned towards the darbar to tell the names of those who had assassinated the Peshwa.

12 ASSASSINATION OF THE PESHWA

Morning of 30 August 1773
Shaniwar Wada, Poona

The eleven-day-long Ganpati festival was on its tenth day. The whole city of Poona was in a religious and festive mood as the festival was approaching its culmination.

Celebrations were planned across the city which was getting ready for Ganpati *Visarjan* – a ritual where the Ganesha idol is immersed in the rivers. One could hear the faint chants of the morning aarti from the Ganpati Rang Mahal of Shaniwar Wada. The Ganpati Rang Mahal was the most decorated palace inside Shaniwar Wada. It housed the musnud and was also the venue for the Ganeshotsav. The palace was decorated with flowers and a large idol of Ganpati was placed in the middle of the long hall on a big platform. The human-size idol was decorated with real gold ornaments. It looked every bit divine. The pandits were reciting the aarti. All present in the palace were in a spiritual mood. Narayanrao Peshwa was in the Ganpati Rang Mahal to attend the morning aarti and to check the preparations for the visarjan.

Once the aarti was over, Narayanrao took the blessings of Lord Ganesha. The pandit gave him a *modak*. Narayanrao Peshwa accepted the prasad and came out of the palace. Haripant Phadke was waiting for him.

"Haripant, you have to ensure that all the preparations for the visarjan are complete by today evening," Narayanrao asked Haripant Phadke, who was in-charge of all the activities for the festival.

"Shrimant, everything is done. I will again check the preparations in the evening before visarjan tomorrow," Haripant confirmed.

Ganeshotsav was an occasion for the Peshwa to celebrate the victories, meet the public and donate generously.

"Where have we reached on the issue of Gardis?" a concerned Narayanrao asked.

"Shrimant, we are discussing with them. We will pay a part of their salaries in the next few days." Haripant Phadke responded. He was not expecting this question from the Peshwa.

"We are under debt and I understand that our financial situation is not very good, but our guards should not suffer because of that. Haripant, ensure that we should address all the issues of Gardis at the earliest," Narayanrao ordered.

Gardis had created ruckus many times inside Shaniwar Wada and it had been a pressing issue for the Peshwa. Haripant had been told to take necessary action, but the financial constraints were such that no amicable solution was found. Narayanrao was not aware of the conspiracy that had been hatched by Raghunathrao with the Gardis.

"Shrimant, we will go to Parvati temple now. Lunch has been arranged there with some dignitaries and the *daanotsav* has been scheduled," said Haripant. As a tradition, Peshwa performed the donations every year during the Ganpati festival.

The Parvati temple was crowded with people who had come for the darshan at the temple and also to get a glimpse of Narayanrao Peshwa on the last day of the puja. Narayanrao reached Parvati temple late in the morning with Haripant Phadke and joined the festivities. The crowd was elated to see the Peshwa and the chants of the aarti echoed in the premises of the temple. The idol of Lord Shiva was decorated with flowers and leaves of *bael.* The smell of incense sticks and the chanting of mantras were making the atmosphere divine. Narayanrao remained in the sanctorum of the temple for some time and then joined the daanotsav.

Peshwa made donations to the brahmins, who had come from various places of religious importance and then joined the public for lunch.

"Shrimant, as you had suggested, *Kesari bhaat* has been prepared for all," Haripant informed him.

The lunch program started at the Parvati temple and Narayanrao joined the dignitaries and public in the festivities. Narayanrao had his lunch and met some people. Once he was done with all the festivities, he got a chance to have a conversation with Raghuji Angre. Raghuji had sent an urgent request for a meeting with the Peshwa a few days back.

"Angre ji, you wanted to meet me and discuss something important?" Narayanrao asked Angre who was camping in Poona. He was waiting to meet the Peshwa. The rumours had spread across Poona and Raghuji had also learned about the conspiracy from his own people who were also in Poona along with him.

"Yes, Shrimant, I wanted to talk to you about something important. Can we speak in private?" Angre requested Peshwa.

As all the formal activities had been completed, Narayanrao and Angre walked to the backside of the Parvati temple and asked for private time.

"Shrimant, I have heard rumours that the Gardis are planning to create ruckus inside Shaniwar Wada and have planned something sinister." Angre spoke with a serious expression on his face.

"You wanted to discuss about Gardis, Angre ji? How come you learned about this?" Narayanrao, who was aware of the situation, did not take the information seriously and smiled. Since his coronation, he had heard many rumours. The initial days were difficult for him, but then the Peshwa learned to live with the rumours and the threats.

"Shrimant, some people from my camp went to the bazaar to buy utensils and other items. During the shopping, they met Gardis who told them that a conspiracy is being hatched to create riots inside Shaniwar Wada. Gardis were very serious about it." Angre sensed that Peshwa was not taking the information seriously, so he emphasized his point again.

"Angre ji, this is not new. Gardis have done this multiple times. I know their problem, but unfortunately, after months it persists. I will ensure that their issues are being taken care of..." Narayanrao comforted Angre and put a hand around his shoulders as they started walking back towards the temple premises.

"Shrimant, there is a threat to your life. It is different this time and rumours are that some of your family members have colluded with Gardis. The riots of Gardis are just a cover-up, a big coup has been planned against you Shrimant," Angre stopped and turned towards Peshwa, looked into his eyes, and spoke with utmost seriousness as his face stiffened.

"Thank you for your concern, Angre ji, I know how these Gardis work. I will ask Haripant to take care of their issues. My family members worked against Dada also and I know they are working against me too. There is nothing new in that." Narayanrao again downplayed the threat to his life and Angre did not press further as they walked to joined the guests.

Shaniwar Wada was decorated for the festival and the preparations for visarjan were in full swing. Narayanrao reached the Ganesh Darwaza of Shaniwar Wada and stopped there for a while to look around. Everything seemed normal to him. It was crowded as usual and there was a lot of activity around due to the festival. It would be very difficult to create a ruckus in such a scenario, thought Narayanrao, the discussion with Angre still fresh in his mind. Gardis had been loyal guards for Shaniwar Wada for years and Narayanrao was not expecting any untoward event during the festive season.

"Haripant, please check that Gardis are paid on time from next month. Angre ji told us that they are very upset with us." Narayanrao spoke to Haripant and shared some details of his interaction with Angre.

"Shrimant, I am going to my Wada and will come in the evening and talk to Gardis." Haripant comforted the Peshwa.

"Angre ji was also talking about some conspiracy being hatched and told that there could be riots again. Invite Nana to my chamber in the evening and we will discuss this in detail," Narayanrao ordered and went to his chamber.

Narayanrao was talking to Haripant while they were at Ganesh

Darwaza and was careless of the fact that guards on duty were close enough to hear any conversation between the two. The news that Angre told him in private, he had shared casually with Haripant at Ganesh Darwaza.

Gardis issues remained pending and there were no focused efforts to resolve their concerns. The senior ministers did not pay any heed to the issues of the guards of Shaniwar Wada. Till that time Gardis were not taken seriously and no one thought that Gardis could dare to touch the Peshwa, the very person they were hired to protect.

The guards who were standing at Ganesh Darwaza eventually overheard the conversation between Narayanrao and Haripant and one of them immediately rushed to meet Sumer Singh Gardi.

"Someone has told them that there could be a ruckus in the Shaniwar Wada soon," the guard told Sumer Singh.

"That is okay, everyone in Poona knows that Gardis are upset with Peshwa," Sumer Singh replied casually.

"Shrimant also told Haripant that there is a chance of riots inside the palace by Gardis and has asked Nana Phadnis to come and meet him in the evening." This statement was shocking for Sumer Singh. He knew that if Nana learns anything about their plan, it would become impossible to do anything after that.

"When did this happen?" Sumer Singh became serious.

"Just now and I came rushing to you," The guard replied.

Sumer Singh sensed that the target had been alerted. He rushed to meet Anandibai and on his way he met Tuloji Pawar.

"What happened Sumer, you look upset?" Tuloji stopped him.

“I am happy to see you here, Sarkar. We are in a difficult situation.” Sumer Singh was puffing and gasping for breath.

“What happened Sumer Singh?” Tuloji took him to a corner in the corridor and whispered in his ear.

“Someone has alerted Shrimant about our plan,” Sumer Singh blurted out.

“What...? How...?”

“Some time back, Shrimant arrived from Parvati temple and at Ganesh Darwaza, he was discussing with Haripant that Gardis would create some ruckus inside Shaniwar Wada soon. He was also talking about some threat to his life.”

“We have to do something, Sumer Singh.” Tuloji was equally shocked to hear that, and it was unsettling for him to learn that Narayanrao had been warned.

“Shrimant ordered Haripant to invite Nana Phadnis in the evening. I am sure he would review the security with his close aides and there might be changes in the guards at the duty.” Sumer Singh told Tuloji.

Tuloji heard what Sumer had just said and took him to an isolated place. He was thinking quickly. If Nana Phadnis would be involved and the security of Narayanrao reviewed, it would become impossible to touch the Peshwa. Nana Phadnis had his informers inside Shaniwar Wada and he would gather all the intelligence. Tuloji realized that it could put his own life at risk.

“Sumer, if we had to execute the plan, it has to be executed now.” Tuloji ordered.

“We are not prepared, Sarkar. We had planned it for later as the Ganpati festival is going-on now and there are many visitors here in Shaniwar Wada. It is not a wise decision to take any action before the visarjan. Should we talk to Vahinisaheb?"

"No, Sumer. There is no need to talk to Vahinisaheb. You already have the order. If Narayanrao meets Nana Phadnis and they plan his defense, we won't be able to do anything. We would be doomed." Tuloji told Sumer Singh, who was equally concerned about the turn of the events.

"I will immediately gather everyone and execute the order," Sumer Singh agreed.

"I am going to talk to Vahinisaheb. I will be in the chamber of Dadasaheb. You finish the work and come there directly. Under any circumstances, you should not leave him alive. If that happens, we all will be dead."

"Ji, Sarkar. I am aware of the consequences." Sumer Singh understood the order and left.

Tuloji went to meet Anandibai and Raghunathrao in their palace. He did not reveal anything about the change in plan to anyone.

A few guards gathered at the Delhi Darwaza of Shaniwar Wada and created a ruckus. Suddenly all gates of Shaniwar Wada were closed, which left many surprised as it was afternoon time. No one was allowed to enter or leave. Some Gardis rushed to the administrative area where clerks were doing their work and killed a few men on their way. A riot-like situation was created inside the palace.

Ichchharam Pant was inside the palace when he saw the guards closing all the gates suddenly and pushing everyone; he sensed that the Gardis were up to something. He rushed to the third floor and dashed to the chamber of Narayanrao to inform him.

"Shrimant, Shrimant..." shouted Ichchharam.

"Stop and kill him..." ordered a Gardi when he heard Ichchharam. He was intercepted by Gardis on the stairs of the first floor. Ichchharam tried to escape and ran to the ground floor into the open ground. As the Gardis followed him, he went into the cowshed. Gardis did not leave him and entered the cowshed. Ichchharam was hiding behind a cow when Gardis entered and the cow started jumping with fear. Gardis tried to control the cow and when they could not, they slaughtered it. The cowshed turned red with the blood of the cow sprayed on the floor and the walls. Ichchharam was dragged out of the cowshed and killed.

Narayanrao was resting in his chamber when he heard the noises from outside. He checked from his window and sensed the trouble. He remembered the conversation he had with Angre earlier in the day. There was a back door in his chamber and from that door, Peshwa rushed to the chamber of Parvatibai.

Narayanrao had always been close to Parvatibai. After Gopikabai left the Shaniwar Wada for Gangapur, Parvatibai was the motherly figure for him in Poona. She had also reciprocated his feelings and treated Narayanrao like her son.

"Kaki... save me, someone is after my life." Parvatibai was also resting when Narayanrao suddenly entered her chamber. He was gasping for breath and scared for his life. She looked at him and sensed the trouble.

"Do not worry, Narayan. Tell me what has happened?" Parvatibai offered him water and tried to calm him down.

"Kaki, Gardis are creating ruckus inside Shaniwar Wada and they are behind our life," Narayanrao blurted out.

Parvatibai tried to gauge the situation from the window of her chamber, but could not gather much information. She could hear some commotion outside, but could not understand the gravity of the situation. Parvatibai was also aware of the ongoing issue with the Gardis, but could not sense the danger.

"I think you should go to your kaka. He would help you." Parvatibai advised Narayanrao.

Narayanrao gulped the water, waited there for a while, and then left for the palace of Raghunathrao. Parvatibai saw him rushing away. As he came into the main corridor on the way to Raghunathrao's palace, the Gardis noticed him.

"*Hujur*, he is here...," shouted a Gardi.

"Come, follow me." Sumer Singh shouted and ran behind Narayanrao.

It was ironic that Peshwa of the Maratha empire was running for his life from his own guards who wanted to kill him. It was ironic that Parvatibai thought that Raghunathrao would be the most suited person to help the Peshwa. It was ironic that Narayanrao too believed that his Kaka would help him. The scene inside Shaniwar Wada was worse than a battlefield. One could not make out who was a friend and who was a foe.

"Catch him!" Sumer Singh ordered the guards who were coming from the other side. Narayanrao was just a few steps away from the chamber of his uncle.

"Kaka, *mala vachva* (save me) ..." Narayanrao was running towards his uncle's palace shouting for help and the Gardis were closing in on him.

Raghunathrao was sitting inside his chamber along with Anandibai and Tuloji Pawar. He had seen the disturbance inside Shaniwar Wada from his window and heard the noises outside.

"What is going on Tuloji?" Raghunathrao asked. He was oblivious to the plan.

"I will go and check. It seems Gardis are creating ruckus again. The irony is, those who protect Shaniwar Wada can't protect their own families." Tuloji said sarcastically and went out.

"Kaka, mala vachva..." Narayanrao entered Raghunathrao's chamber and fell at his feet. Raghunathrao was stunned to see Narayanrao in such a helpless situation. Sumer Singh and Khadak Singh followed with guards behind them.

"Narayan, what happened?" Raghunathrao sat on the floor near Narayanrao, put his hand on his nephew's shoulder, and asked in a concerned voice. Anandibai was standing just behind him thinking that her plan was about to reach its climax.

"Kaka, they will kill me. Please save me..." Narayanrao pleaded with his uncle with folded hands, tears running down his cheeks. The Peshwa was lying on the floor at the feet of his uncle and was begging for help.

"No one will touch you in my presence, Narayan. Don't worry!" Raghunathrao spoke loudly; everyone around looked at each other in confusion.

"Kaka, I don't want to be the Peshwa. You take the Peshwai and I will retire from all my duties. Please spare my life, Kaka." Narayanrao pleaded again.

"No one will harm you here, Narayan." Raghunathrao got up, took out his sword, and announced to everyone's surprise. Tuloji Pawar was also back in the chamber.

"Sarkar, we have to follow our orders." Sumer Singh said and marched towards Narayanrao; he was unable to understand Raghunathrao's behaviour.

"Sumer Singh... Stop!" Raghunathrao thundered.

The atmosphere inside the chamber was charged. Sumer Singh was in a dilemma of what to do. Anandibai and Tuloji Pawar were looking towards Raghunathrao, who was standing firmly to protect his nephew.

Anandibai was calm at that moment and decided to take charge. She knew her husband would not listen to anyone else.

"Sumer Singh, you have to follow your orders," Anandibai said authoritatively and then looked towards her husband, who slowly lowered his sword.

"Kaka, save me kaka. Don't leave me. They will kill me, kaka." Narayanrao pleaded again as he saw his uncle receding.

"Hujur, I can't take risk of leaving him alive now. I don't want to put my life and your life at risk," Sumer Singh told Raghunathrao, but did not get any response.

"Swari, try to understand. Let the Gardis settle this and you stay out." Anandibai went close to Raghunathrao, touched his hand which had the sword, and signalled him to put back his sword.

"Kaka, please kaka..." Narayanrao was pleading.

Raghunathrao was caught between love for his nephew and greed for power. Greed won. Raghunathrao lowered his sword and took a step back. Anandibai signalled Sumer Singh, who caught a leg of Narayanrao and pulled him. Narayanrao was still holding the feet of Raghunathrao.

"Kaka, mala vachva. You take the Peshwai kaka, please spare my life, kaka. I will go to Gangapur and stay with aai." Narayanrao pleaded for help for the last time. As Sumer Singh and Khadak Singh pulled him, his grip loosened.

Chafaji Tilekar was following Narayanrao and somehow after fighting guards on the way reached the chamber with two dasis.

"Shrimant, Shrimant..." Chafaji was stunned to see the way Narayanrao was being manhandled by Sumer Singh and his Gardis.

"Stay away from him..." thundered Sumer Singh.

Sensing that there was immediate danger to the life of the Peshwa, Chafaji fell on Narayanrao to protect him by covering him with his body and both the dasis followed him.

"Sumer Singh, you are wasting your time now!" Tuloji commented.

Chafaji was the first to be pulled away and Khadak Singh's sword separated his head from his body. There was blood all over the floor. Then the guards pulled away both the dasis and killed them. Sumer Singh pulled Narayanrao Peshwa with the help of Khadak Singh and other guards. Sumer Singh pierced his heart with his sword and soon blood started rushing down his body. Khadak Singh wanted to take no chance. With Sumer Singh, he cut the body of Peshwa into pieces.

The Peshwa of the Maratha empire was killed in broad daylight inside his capital palace by his own guards in the presence of his uncle and aunt.

"Shrimant, the task is complete," Sumer Singh declared.

Raghunathrao went numb. His sword slipped from his hand making a minor cut in it and he too fell on his seat with shock.

"Long live Shrimant Raghunathrao Peshwa!" shouted Sumer Singh and the other guards followed. Sumer Singh cut his thumb with his sword and as a symbolic gesture of victory applied his blood on the forehead of Raghunathrao.

Anandibai was elated. Her plan had been successfully executed.

"Swari, now you would become Peshwa," declared Anandibai and handed over her gold necklace to Sumer Singh who left with his guards to control the situation outside.

The Gardis went on a rampage inside Shaniwar Wada and looted whatever they could gather. All the gates of Shaniwar Wada were already closed to outsiders.

The Maratha capital palace and Peshwai were under siege.

13 THE FUNERAL

Trimbakrao could not hold himself. In a blink of an eye, he had collapsed on the floor of Raghunathrao's chamber. The floor of the chamber had turned red with the blood of the Peshwa and others who were brutally murdered while protecting the Peshwa. There were four dead bodies inside the chamber which were butchered so mercilessly that body parts were mingled and lying everywhere. It was difficult to identify which body part belonged to whom. The Gardis did not allow them to touch or move anything.

It was a terrible sight inside Raghunathrao's chamber. Trimbakrao could not believe what had happened inside that chamber. When he regained composure, he asked for a cloth to cover the body parts of the deceased.

Trimbakrao and Nana Phadnis had no idea what had transpired in this chamber. Nana Phadnis had heard many rumours for the past few months. He was regretting the fact that he had not taken it seriously. Nana was worried about the consequences the assassination of the Peshwa would have on the Maratha empire and the message it would send to both allies and enemies. Both were speechless and it took them a while to gauge the seriousness of the situation.

"How did this happen, Dadasaheb?" Nana Phadnis gathered the courage to ask the difficult question.

"Everything has been destroyed, Nana... we have lost our Narayan." Raghunathrao responded. They again went silent for a while, staring at the blood-stained floor of the chamber and the body parts of the Peshwa and three others. The white cotton cloth, which was used to cover the body parts, had slowly lost its whiteness and turned red, conveying the brutality of the crime that had been committed.

It was easy to plan a campaign against an enemy, make a strategy for the war, and fight on the battle ground. Nana was helpless about the situation at Shaniwar Wada where the Peshwa had been assassinated in cold blood and he had no questions to ask and no victims to interrogate and punish. He couldn't think straight; his mind went numb. The assassination of the Peshwa inside Shaniwar Wada was a kind of act that would be remembered whenever Maratha history would be written. A family dispute could take such an ugly turn, Dadasaheb could stoop so low to get power – he had never imagined.

"We have to prepare for the last rites of Narayanrao," said Trimbakrao and he went out of the chamber to ask for some help.

The Gardis had taken charge of the Shaniwar Wada and were controlling every movement inside the palace. Nana Phadnis realized that they needed to perform the last rites of the Peshwa first and for that, they need the support of Gardis. Any negotiation, truce, or confrontation could be planned later.

"I will take care of the last rites of everyone; you don't have to worry about anything." Sumer Singh pushed Trimbakrao back to the chamber and did not entertain his request when he tried to go out to make arrangements for the funeral.

Trimbakrao and Nana Phadnis were two of the most respected ministers in the Maratha empire and on a normal day, a Gardi would not have dared to even talk to them, but the situation had changed so much that Sumer Singh did not even allow them to go outside of the chamber to arrange the last rites of Narayanrao. Nana had sensed that the power equation inside the palace had suddenly changed and this was not possible without the support of Raghunathrao. Nana thought that it was wise to follow the new power order and avoid any confrontation.

"Dadasaheb, Shrimant deserves proper last rites. I can't see his dead body lying scattered here on the floor. We are seeking permission from a security guard to perform the last rites of the Peshwa," Nana Phadnis said firmly.

Raghunathrao listened and realizing the sensitivity of the matter, nodded towards Sumer Singh, who reluctantly ordered servants for help. Trimbakrao got busy with servants for the last rites and Nana Phadnis planned to go out and inform everyone.

"Dadasaheb, we will leave now to make necessary preparations for the last rites of Shrimant Narayanrao and also to share this tragic news with everyone outside as no one is aware of what has happened here. Various rumours are floating around, which is not good for anyone," said Nana Phadnis in a terse tone.

"If you go out now, you won't be allowed to come inside again. As it is already late, all the rituals would be performed tomorrow only," Sumer Singh declared.

Nana looked toward Sumer Singh and stared straight at him. They did not say anything, but the message was passed. Nana's silence conveyed to him that, as a Gardi, he should know his limits. Trimbakrao and Nana Phadnis went out of Raghunathrao's chamber, this time Sumer Singh did not stop them.

"Nana, you can tell everyone outside that in the riots inside the palace, we have lost Narayanrao. Tell them that Gangabai, Parvatibai, and we all are safe." Raghunathrao advised Nana, who had already decided what information he would share with whom once he was out of the palace.

"Nana, you leave and make necessary plans. I will stay here till the last rites are performed," Trimbakrao said as he could not trust anyone anymore. He was worried that if Gardis could arrange the murder of the Peshwa, they could arrange the disposal of the dead body also.

"No one is allowed to stay here; you have to leave immediately." Sumer Singh thundered.

"I will stay here Sumer Singh and for that, I don't need permission from you or anyone else in this palace. If you force me to leave, for that you have to kill me and then you can send my dead body out, or mix with these bodies and cremate it," Trimbakrao said in a loud voice. Raghunathrao agreed to let him stay and Sumer Singh did not press further.

It was a long walk for Nana from Raghunathrao's chamber to Ganesh Darwaza. On his way, he again looked around the palace. It was already dark and very little light was there inside the palace. Despite that, he could figure out the impact of the riots. Riots at this scale were certainly well planned and executed from the highest level inside Shaniwar Wada.

When Nana came out, everyone was eagerly waiting for him. Nana told them about the incident inside the palace and with Haripant Phadke, he went to meet Ram Shastri, who had left for his house by then. As a crime was committed inside the palace, it was important to inform and involve the Chief Justice of the empire.

It was late in the night when Nana Phadnis reached the house of Ram Shastri. He had slept by then. Nana repeatedly knocked on the door. After some time, Janaki opened the door and welcomed Nana and Haripant inside. Nana sat on the bed and did not speak for a while; he was finding it difficult to search for the right words to break this dreadful news to Ram Shastri.

"Hope Shrimant is safe, Nana?" a concerned Ram Shastri asked.

"Marathas have done a Mughal act, Shastribuwa. My fears have finally come true." Nana replied in a trembling voice staring at the diya which was lighted in a far corner of the house.

"What are you saying? Please tell me how is Shrimant?" Ram Shastri asked again, sensing the sadness in Nana's voice.

"Shrimant has been killed by the Gardis in the riots today, inside the palace," Nana told Ram Shastri, his throat choked.

Ram Shastri listened to the news and went numb for a while. Janaki too joined the conversation. She was stunned when she heard the news of Narayanrao's murder.

"What are you saying, Nana? Are you sure?" Ram Shastri could not believe what he had heard.

"Yes, Shastribuwa. We all are the witnesses to the most shameful incident in the history of Marathas. It has been the worst coup that one could imagine. There were riots inside the palace. The Gardis went on a rampage. With Shrimant they have killed ten more and slaughtered a cow also. The palace has been polluted today, Shastribuwa." Nana was almost crying.

Ram Shastri could not digest the news. He sat on the floor with a thud and held his head in his hands. Nana remained silent for a while and then asked the difficult question.

"Tomorrow would be the last rites of Shrimant. We have to make all the preparations for that and have to ensure that there are no more riots anywhere." Nana was pragmatic.

Ram Shastri did not say anything. He had no words. With the help of Nana, Janaki took him to the bed. Nana and Haripant went back to the palace and fortified the palace from outside to stop anyone from leaving the Shaniwar Wada.

"We have to be ready for the worst, Haripant. Get ready with all your troops by morning." Nana told Haripant who decided to camp outside the Shaniwar Wada for the night.

Inside the Shaniwar Wada, Gangabai was inconsolable. She was in Ganpati Rang Mahal and was checking the preparations for visarjan when the riots broke. By the time, she reached her chamber, Narayanrao was not there. She frantically searched for him everywhere, but could not gather any news of him. Parvatibai had come to her chamber and told her that Narayan had come to her asking her help. In turn, she had asked him to go to Raghunathrao. Kamla went on to check, but she was not allowed anywhere near Raghunathrao's chamber. Kamla risked her life and went close to Sumer Singh to gather some information, but could not succeed. As the time passed, the news spread across Shaniwar Wada and she overheard the Gardis.

It was Kamla who first told Parvatibai about the incident. When Gangabai heard the news, she rushed out of her chamber to the chamber of Raghunathrao, but was stopped on her way.

"You can't go out..." a guard on duty told her.

"I have to go and see Swari, just let me go," Gangabai pleaded.

The guard instructed a dasi who took her inside and the gate of her chamber was closed.

It was a long and dreadful night in Poona and the dawn was still far away.

Ram Shastri was unable to sleep. He was thinking about the promise he had made to Madhavrao and was distraught that he could not keep his promise. Nana Phadnis was fully awake and was thinking about a looming political crisis that could put the lives of many and the future of Marathas at stake. Haripant Phadke was outside the Shaniwar Wada with his troops, alert for any activity from inside.

The Gardis were guarding the Shaniwar Wada with all the gates still closed and were on continuous vigil. Kamla was sitting with Gangabai who was still crying to get a last glimpse of her dead husband. Parvatibai had retired to her room and was looking out of her window, blaming herself for advising Narayanrao to go to Raghunathrao for help. Anandibai was in her chamber waiting for the right time to fully execute her plan. When she sensed that the night had fallen enough, she sent a message to Sumer Singh.

Sumer Singh was still on duty. It had been a long night for him also, but he was not tired. He was continuously visiting all the gates of the palace and giving instructions to the guards. It must be around midnight when he was asked to visit Raghunathrao's chamber. As he arrived, he saw that Anandibai was waiting for him.

She was standing at the entrance of her chamber. Sumer Singh saluted to her and she responded meekly. Her face was expressionless and she was deep in thoughts.

"Hujur..." Sumer Singh said after a while when she did not say anything. Anandibai turned to him.

"I was thinking about the funeral, Sumer. I am sure Nana and Trimbakrao would make grand plans for it. If the funeral of Narayan becomes a public affair, it can create sympathy for him. We can't wait till morning for the funeral. This funeral must be a private affair and I don't want any problems later." Anandibai told Sumer Singh.

"What do you want?" Sumer Singh agreed with her thoughts.

"We have to close this chapter forever. I don't want the involvement of anyone else in this. I am sure that Nana and Ram Shastri would not sleep tonight. They would be making some plans for tomorrow. I don't want any of their plans to succeed. Narayanrao's last rites have to be performed now," Anandibai ordered.

"In the middle of the night?" asked a surprised Sumer Singh as the Hindu tradition was that generally funerals were performed during the daytime only.

"Yes, in the middle of the night," Anandibai confirmed her order. The traditions no more mattered to her.

"Haripant Phadke had his troops are deployed on every gate of the palace. We can't go out to perform the funeral," Sumer Singh told her about the situation outside the palace.

"I don't know how you will manage this Sumer, but the last rites have to be done before the sun rises." Anandibai ordered again.

It must be past midnight, still there was time for Poona to wake up and prepare for the Ganpati visarjan. Trimbakrao was sitting on the floor near the body of Narayanrao on the ground floor of Shaniwar Wada waiting for the long and dark night to end.

"What are you doing?" a stunned Trimbakrao asked the Gardis when they lifted the body of Narayanrao.

"We have orders to perform the last rites of everyone immediately," said Sumer Singh and then he asked Trimbakrao to cooperate with them.

"You can't perform a funeral in the middle of the night!" Trimbakrao objected.

Sumer instructed the Gardis and they surrounded Trimbakrao. Sumer Singh again requested him to cooperate. Trimbakrao had no choice and he knew that if he did not cooperate, they would still go ahead and perform the last rites.

Before dawn, the cremation of Narayanrao Peshwa took place on the bank of the Mutha river near Shaniwar Wada. By the time Poona saw the first ray of the sun and the visarjan started, the ashes of Narayanrao were submerged in the water of the Mutha river.

Gangabai was told about the cremation of Narayanrao later in the day. She was not even given the chance of being sati. There was no reaction from her to the news; she remained on her bed like a stone. Her tears had not stopped since the time she heard about the murder of her husband. Kamla was sitting close to her.

A batik and the wife of a Peshwa were in the same situation. They were helpless.

The gates of Shaniwar Wada remained closed the whole day and no visitors were permitted by Raghunathrao, who had decided to take charge of all administrative activities of the empire immediately. The news of the murder of the Peshwa had stunned everyone in Poona and spread like wildfire across the Maratha empire from south to north.

Nana Phadnis was confident that Raghunathrao would try to declare himself as the next Peshwa. He was at his house and was writing letters and dispatching to all the Maratha allies to inform them about the news and also garner support against Raghunathrao. When he was done writing letters, he decided to visit Sakharam Bapu to take him to his side. After reaching Sakharam Bapu's house, he learned that Sakharam Bapu had not come back home since yesterday afternoon.

Nana Phadnis thought about Sakharam Bapu, the most trusted advisor of Raghunathrao and an astute politician. Raghunathrao would certainly need the services of Sakharam Bapu at such times and he would have invited him. Nana Phadnis had planned to meet Sakharam Bapu and stop him from meeting Raghunathrao. The absence of Sakharam Bapu from his house confirmed his fears.

Nana Phadnis thought that Raghunathrao might have called him to Shaniwar Wada. So, he rushed to the palace.

"Did you see Bapu entering the palace yesterday?" he asked Haripant.

"The only time gate of Shaniwar Wada opened was when you entered and came out." Haripant responded. They were guarding all the entry points of the palace. Nana Phadnis thought for a while, that Sakharam Bapu was neither at his home nor with Raghunathrao.

"Sakharam Bapu is being given the task of managing things outside the palace. I am sure he has left to talk to the allies." Nana Phadnis told him.

"If he would have left, someone would have noted."

"But he is not traceable!" Nana was puzzled by his absence.

14 THE POWER TUSSLE

It was dreary in the town of Gangapur as the news of the tragic death of the Peshwa had reached there. Everyone in the town was grieving with Gopikabai. Gopikabai had given birth to three sons, but fate had been cruel to her. In a period of twelve years, she had lost her husband and three sons. She was so grief-stricken that she stopped eating anything and roamed around Gangapur begging for the food from door to door. People felt her pain and sometimes would walk with her, and give her food and clothes. Gopikabai ate whatever she would get as alms, her weight dropped significantly and her body became frail. The royal sheen from her face was completely washed out. The news hit her so badly that she lost her senses.

Gopikabai had always been ambitious and wanted the Peshwai for her sons. Two of her sons did become Peshwas and she tried to assert control over the activities of the state through them. The ambitious plans of Gopikabai did succeed, but her cousin, Anandibai had to struggle to fulfill her ambitions. As Gopikabai lost her family and her senses, Anandibai was slowly getting hold of the power.

Raghunathrao's chamber had become the new power centre of the Maratha empire.

"Chinto, yesterday I asked you to inform Bapu to come and meet me. What happened?" Raghunathrao asked Chinto Vitthal.

As Nana had expected, Raghunathrao was looking for his most trusted advisor.

"Dadasaheb, I did send a message, but Bapu is not at his house for the last two days." Chinto responded.

"Where would he go?" asked a puzzled Raghunathrao.

"There are rumours that Bapu is missing. No one has seen him in the last two days." Chinto told him.

Raghunathrao was in his chamber with Chinto Vitthal, Moroba Phadnis and Bhavanrao Pratinidhi. He was planning his next move. Sakharam Bapu, his most trusted advisor, was missing. Nana Phadnis and Ram Shastri had not approached him or tried to come and meet him after that day. Raghunathrao quickly wanted to take charge of the empire and declare himself the Peshwa to suppress any uprising against him. Sakharam Bapu could have been a big help in such a situation.

"Bhavanrao, write a letter and ask Lakshman to send that message to Mudhoji today. Inform him that he should immediately march with his army towards Poona. We have to plan for any untoward situation that could arise. I know that Nana, Haripant, Trimbakrao and Shastribuwa would not sit idle." Raghunathrao was making plans to counter any armed action against him.

"Nana Phadnis is a big danger, Dadasaheb. Shouldn't we put him under house arrest?" Chinto suggested.

"This is not the right time for such actions Chinto. We want public sympathy also, which we don't have. If we perform such an act, the public will never be with us. Nana has his supporters."

"We have managed so far by fortifying the Shaniwar Wada. What if someone tries to trap us inside and surround the Shaniwar

Wada from all sides?" Chinto was worried that if a parallel power develops in the empire, Shaniwar Wada would be an easy target.

"I will think about it," responded Raghunathrao.

Haider and Nizam were the immediate danger for Raghunathrao and an army from Mudhoji would be a big support, but he had still not thought about moving out of Shaniwar Wada. If any of his opponents could gather support from allies, Raghunathrao could easily be trapped inside and his dream of becoming Peshwa would be crashed. The formal decision of succession had to be made quickly.

It was not wise to conduct a darbar in such a scenario and discuss the subject of succession. Raghunathrao feared that there might be opinions against him. The Gardis were becoming another issue for him. They were continuously demanding to settle their dues which he could not, due to financial constraints. Raghunathrao had ordered Bhavanrao to talk to Sumer Singh and bargain some time with him.

* * *

"Shastribuwa, we have come here to take your advice." Nana Phadnis told Ram Shastri when they reached his house with Trimbakrao and Haripant.

"The way things are changing in the empire, Nana, I am not sure if I could be of any help," replied Ram Shastri.

"Shastribuwa, the Maratha throne is empty. Dadasaheb is the only heir in the family now. It is evident by his actions that he will take charge. Do you think considering what has happened on that day, he is the right choice for the Peshwai?" asked Nana.

"Do you believe that Dadasaheb was involved in this?" Ram Shastri questioned Nana.

"Shastribuwa, I was there the whole night on that day. Dadasaheb showed no emotions, he was not sad. Narayan's dead body was lying in his chamber. Who else could be involved?" Trimbakrao responded to the question asked by Ram Shastri.

"We all know about Dadasaheb and his intentions, but we should not make any conclusion in haste. I understand the importance of political continuity at this stage, but I don't want to be a part of any political matter. I would focus on the investigation and if you want to discuss the incidents of that day, I would be eager to know more," Ram Shastri cleared his position on the subject.

"If Dadasaheb takes charge, will you support him?" asked Nana as he was not comfortable with the neutral stand taken by the Chief justice.

"Nana, I am more concerned about justice to Shrimant Narayanrao. Anything related to succession or political activity can be taken care of by all of you. I would be happy if I am not involved in the matter of politics." Ram Shastri responded.

He was frustrated by the way things were proceeding at that time. The Marathas were divided into two camps. To his surprise, both the camps wanted to take charge of the political activities. It seemed to him that he was the only one who was concerned about the murder of the Peshwa and the investigation.

"Shastribuwa, you are the chief justice of the empire. We will wait for the conclusion of your investigation. Till then, we will not join Dadasaheb in state affairs." Trimbakrao told him.

The final prayers to pay the last homage to Narayanrao Peshwa were planned on the tenth day after the demise. All the dignitaries were present on the shore of the Mutha river. Once all the rituals were done, Nana Phadnis along with Trimbakrao, Sakharam Bapu, Haripant, Patwardhan, and Ram Shastri decided that they will not participate in any activity of the Maratha empire and will not support the coronation of Raghunathrao.

"We should not support any activity till Shastribuwa finishes his investigation." Nana Phadnis shared his thoughts as they were discussing their next steps.

"We can stay away from all affairs, but Dadasaheb would certainly take charge of the empire. I have heard that he was planning to visit Satara to get the robes of the Peshwa," Trimbakrao told the group.

There were discussions of a parallel government being formed against Raghunathrao, but the biggest challenge for this group was that they had no one to lead them. The powerful post of Peshwa, which had been in the Bhat family for long, needed someone to hold it, even if that was just symbolic.

Raghunathrao seemed a natural choice at the moment and he was already acting like the Peshwa.

Ram Shastri did not say anything. His investigation was running parallelly though Raghunathrao had expressed his displeasure on the investigation. As the investigation proceeded, getting a witness was a daunting task for Ram Shastri. It was a known fact that when Narayanrao was killed, Raghunathrao was present inside Shaniwar Wada, but no witness came forward who had confessed to seeing the actual crime.

As Raghunathrao started asserting control over the activities of the empire, the Poona public was getting jittery. Rumours were rife that he had killed his nephew. A murderer taking charge of the Maratha empire was unsettling for the ministers and subjects of the empire. Ram Shastri was under pressure for a fair and fast trial, but he had very limited progress.

"Shastribuwa..." Janaki heard someone calling her husband and knocking on the door, she went to check.

"Kamla, please come..." Janaki welcomed Kamla to her house.

"You look unwell Kamla." Janaki asked her, but she did not respond.

"Kamla, what happened?" Ram Shastri asked her.

He had not met Kamla after that incident in the court when slave practice was banned, but he had seen her many times with Gangabai in the chamber of Narayanrao.

"You are asking me this, don't you already know, Shastribuwa? Even a child in the Maratha empire knows what had happened on that day inside Shaniwar Wada," Kamla said sarcastically. Kamla had become a devotee of Gangabai and after the murder of Narayanrao, she could not see her in pain.

"What do you mean?" asked Ram Shastri.

"You are the Chief Justice of the Maratha empire and you are asking me the meaning?"

"Kamla, you are crossing your limits," Ram Shastri spoke in a loud voice.

"They crossed all limits of inhumanity inside Shaniwar Wada on that day and you are telling this poor, helpless, and illiterate woman that she is crossing limits, Shastribuwa?" Kamla was unfazed and spoke fearlessly.

"Please tell me clearly what you want?" Ram Shastri controlled his temper and asked again.

"I want justice from you, Shastribuwa."

Kamla told everything to Ram Shastri about the happenings of that day. He listened patiently. After she was done talking, she started crying.

"I have heard this many times since that day Kamla, but justice can't be delivered based on rumours and emotions. It needs proof to convict a person for a crime." Ram Shastri responded.

"I always used to curse myself for being born poor. I thought I was illiterate and helpless, but today I thank god for being like this. What is the use of being literate, knowledgeable, powerful, and influential if you can't stand against injustice, Shastribuwa! I had come to you with some expectations and if you too can't do anything, no one in this empire would."

"Kamla, I am helpless..." Ram Shastri replied.

"So is that woman who had lost her husband! She did not even get a chance to see him one last time. Worst still, she was not even given a choice to be sati. No one cares about that unfortunate widow and the child which she is carrying in her womb."

"What did you say, is Vahinisaheb...?" Ram Shastri stopped as he thought it was inappropriate to ask that directly.

"I will get a proof for you, Shastribuwa," said Kamla and walked out of the house.

Janaki rushed behind her to confirm the news of Gangabai's pregnancy.

When Kamla reached Shaniwar Wada, she had a clear target in her mind, Sumer Singh Gardi. Kamla had observed on a few occasions that whenever she saw him, he always stared at her with lustful eyes. She thought this could make her life easy, but she did not want to raise any suspicion and followed his activity closely, as he was frequently visiting Raghunathrao's chamber.

* * *

"Dadasaheb, it is difficult to convince Sumer Singh now. He wants full settlement along with the fort of Purandar," Bhavanrao told Raghunathrao.

"He has already received two lakh rupees. We have promised that once Swari becomes Peshwa, we will fulfill our promise," Anandibai replied to Bhavanrao.

"He is getting impatient and wants to settle everything at the earliest. I have called him to meet you as I could not convince him of anything," Bhavanrao explained the situation to Anandibai this time as Raghunathrao was still lost in thoughts.

"We don't have much money in the treasury at the moment and can't pay Sumer Singh," Raghunathrao responded in a calm, but concerned tone.

"Don't worry, I will find a way," Anandibai was frustrated with the behaviour of Sumer Singh, but she did not want to upset him at that time and was waiting for an opportune moment. As they were discussing a possible solution, the guard announced the arrival of Sumer Singh.

"Sumer Singh, you are aware of the situation of the treasury. You have been paid two lakh rupees. When Swari becomes Peshwa, we will fulfill our promise," Anandibai welcomed Sumer Singh and tried to pacify him.

"Vahinisaheb, I have delivered what I promised to you. Now, you should deliver what you promised to me. I can't wait till eternity. I know the risks to my life now," demanded Sumer Singh.

"There is no risk to your life, Sumer Singh." Bhavanrao tried to comfort him.

"I am giving you a few more days to give me the money and the fort of Purandar. If I do not get my money then Dadasaheb may not get the throne." Sumer Singh challenged Anandibai.

"What do you mean, Sumer Singh?" Anandibai was furious by his statement, but tried to control her emotions. She asked him politely.

"Dadasaheb is not the only heir alive in the Peshwa family. Don't forget that Ali Bahadur is alive and the public will be happier if he becomes the Peshwa." Sumer Singh threatened them and left without saying anything further.

He was rushing through the corridor of Shaniwar Wada and was about to reach his chamber when suddenly Kamla emerged from nowhere and ran into him. Both of them fell on the floor together with Kamla falling over him, intentionally.

Sumer Singh looked at her face and blushed; she responded with a flirtatious smile. She had succeeded in her first step.

* * *

Nana Phadnis was sitting in his house, alone. Raghunathrao was already managing the administrative affairs of the state and had not invited him or other senior ministers to the darbar. At that time the affairs of the state were not his prime concern; he was concerned about the safety of Gangabai and her child. The news came as a big relief for the group which was opposing Raghunathrao. If Gangabai gives birth to a son, he could be the legal heir of Peshwai. Nana Phadnis had invited Haripant to his house to discuss the safety of Gangabai.

"I don't think it would be safe for Vahinisaheb to stay in Shaniwar Wada anymore. We should find a safe place for her where she can stay till the birth of the child." Nana told Haripant.

"What do you have in mind?" Haripant asked him.

"I think the Purandar fort will be a safe option for her to stay. I will talk to Patwardhan about this, but you start preparing for her departure. You will remain in charge of her safety till the birth of the child and will stay at Purandar fort only."

As Nana was worried about the safety of Gangabai, Anandibai was also worried about the arrival of a legal heir to Narayanrao. Anandibai wanted that Raghunathrao should officially take the charge of the empire at the earliest. She would have more power once her husband became Peshwa and could then take care of Gangabai and the child in her womb.

"When are you going to Satara to get the robes of the Peshwa?" she asked Raghunathrao.

"I am still thinking about it. I feel it would be good to wait for some time."

"Any wait now would prove very costly. If Gangabai gives birth to a son, I am sure he would be projected as the next Peshwa," said Anandibai.

"How can a new-born child become Peshwa?" Raghunathrao laughed at her statement.

"Just for the namesake, so that these ministers can rule freely." Anandibai had sensed the activities of the opposition group and the chances of a revolt.

"Don't worry about the child."

"Yes, I will take care of the child." Anandibai told her husband.

She had already made a secret plan with Tuloji Pawar.

Bhavanrao was concerned when he arrived at the camp of Raghunathrao. His discussion with Sumer Singh had not yielded any results. The Gardis were pressurizing that their demands be fulfilled, else they would not support Raghunathrao for the Peshwai and would declare Ali Bahadur as the next Peshwa. It was a difficult situation for Raghunathrao who had already left his palace in Shaniwar Wada and was camping on the outskirts of Poona to avoid any potential threat of siege of the palace.

"What should we do in such a situation, Bhavanrao? You are close to him. Why don't you talk to Sumer Singh and Khadak Singh?" Raghunathrao asked for advice.

"There is no point in talking to them, Dadasaheb. They won't listen to anyone now. All they want is their money. I have already talked to them about the forts and they have agreed to accept money instead of the forts. So now we have to pay them three lakh rupees more for the forts."

"That is a big amount, Bhavanrao; the treasury is still not in our control. We can sell some royal jewellery, but not now." Raghunathrao was worried about the settlements with the Gardis.

His concern was that Shaniwar Wada was still under control of Gardis and he was camping outside. Gardis had all the power and they could declare Ali Bahadur as the next Peshwa. Ali Bahadur was the son of Shamsher Bahadur and the grandson of Bajirao and Mastani. He had garnered strong sympathy within the Maratha empire after the death of his father in the battle of Panipat.

"Shrimant, Visaji Krishna would be arriving from north in a few days. I will ensure that as soon as he comes, he should meet you first." Bhavanrao told Raghunathrao.

In the chaos that followed the murder, everyone had forgotten that Narayanrao had sent Visaji on a campaign to the north. As

Raghunathrao was camping on the outskirts of Poona, he jumped on the opportunity.

* * *

Raghunathrao was staying outside Shaniwar Wada to capture the power and avoid any conflict with the group which was not supporting him. Anandibai was managing the politics from her chamber inside the palace. The news of Gangabai's pregnancy had hit her hard. She was aware that this would only give hope to the opposition camp which was led by Nana Phadnis. Nana had already made his intentions clear of not supporting Raghunathrao's claim to power. The group led by Nana Phadnis was still working in secrecy and Raghunathrao had no inkling of an immediate revolt by his ministers.

Anandibai was contemplating her next steps when the guard announced the arrival of Tuloji Pawar.

"Vahinisaheb! What is the problem? You called me urgently?" Tuloji asked her.

Anandibai did not speak for a while and signalled Tuloji to sit. He followed as instructed and they remained silent for some time.

"You are worried about something?" Tuloji asked again when she did not speak for long. Anandibai stared at him. Her eyes penetrated his body like she was looking past him, into the future.

"After Narayanrao, there is only one legal heir to the Peshwai. There is a possibility that many ministers might not support Swari, but due to a lack of options, they will be left with no choice. This would be a simple political need that would compel the Maratha chiefs and allies to support him. However, the situation will change once Gangabai gives birth to a child." Anandibai spoke seriously.

Tuloji was not aware of Gangabai's pregnancy. When he heard it, it did not bother him much. Even if Gangabai gave birth to a son, he would not claim the throne immediately after birth.

"Once Dadasaheb takes charge, you will control everything, Vahinisaheb."

"It is not that easy, Tuloji. This child can become a big pain for Swari."

"What do you suggest then?" Tuloji gave up and asked about her plan.

"We need to eliminate any future claimant of Peshwai," Anandibai said in a calm voice.

Tuloji was stunned to hear such a statement from her. He knew that she meant what she said. The murder of Narayanrao had caused a huge uproar in the empire and at such time, the murder of his pregnant widow would be detrimental to their purpose.

"We should not take any such steps for the next few months, Vahinisaheb. Let Dadasaheb take charge and things settle down a bit. We can take care of the child after that," Tuloji told her.

On the other hand, as the news of Gangabai's pregnancy reached Nana Phadnis, his resolve to stand against Raghunathrao grew stronger. He called Ram Shastri, Trimbakrao, and Haripant for a meeting.

'The birth of this child could change the future of the empire,' thought Nana Phadnis, the leader in him was slowly taking the centre stage in Maratha politics.

THE PROOF 15

The Maratha empire was in turmoil and so was the life of Sakharam Bapu after the murder of Narayanrao Peshwa. He was grief-stricken since the day he had heard the news.

Sakharam Bapu had been an astute politician who had the experience of running the administrative affairs of the empire and also running a war campaign. He was a part of many campaigns for the Marathas during the reigns of Nanasaheb and on many occasions had accompanied Raghunathrao on these campaigns. It was during these campaigns that Sakharam Bapu developed a strong rapport with Raghunathrao and became his ardent supporter and loyalist. When Madhavrao took charge, Sakharam Bapu was removed from his post for some time. However, Madhavrao respected him for his wisdom and experience and he again became a prominent minister during the reigns of Madhavrao. Sakharam Bapu always remained a close confidant of Raghunathrao.

Many conspiracies were floating around Shaniwar Wada during the reigns of Narayanrao. Sakharam Bapu had also heard rumours about the coup before the murder of Peshwa, but he never paid any heed. The murder of Narayanrao inside the Shaniwar Wada was a shock to Sakharam Bapu. For a few days, he was untraceable and many in the empire believed that he had supported Raghunathrao in the act and had run away after the incident.

Raghunathrao desperately needed him in such times as Bapu was his most trusted advisor and a staunch supporter. Nana was also searching for him, but he had not heard anything for a few days. One day after the morning aarti, a royal pandit from the Maratha darbar noticed him sitting on the pavements of Parvati temple in a dishevelled condition. Sakharam Bapu was begging for food outside the temple.

"Bapu?"

Bapu nodded to convey that he had heard his name, but did not move. Pandit looked at him and informed the passersby. As the news of his disappearance had spread through Poona, immediately a crowd gathered around him. Many in the crowd had recognized him. As the news spread further through the city, Nana Phadnis himself arrived at the temple and arranged his travel back to his house.

Sakharam Bapu had sensed the intentions of Raghunathrao and his greed for power, but he never believed that Raghunathrao could take such a step. When the news of Narayanrao's murder reached him, he was deeply hurt. It was a matter of utter shame for him that the Peshwa was killed by his guards and he being the senior-most minister could not even sense the danger. He could not sleep for the whole night on that day and sometime just before dawn, he left his house and walked around the city for days and begged for food.

"Please take rest Bapu, we will speak after a few days," Nana told him once they reached his place.

"We have lost Shrimant," Bapu responded. Nana realized that the incident had left a deep mental scar on Bapu. Nana needed the support of Bapu against Raghunathrao, but it was not the right time to discuss politics.

"Shastribuwa is investigating the incident Bapu," Nana replied.

* * *

Ram Shastri had been a regular visitor to Shaniwar Wada, but after the death of Narayanrao, he had visited the palace only a few times. During his investigation into the murder of Narayanrao, he faced strong resistance from Raghunathrao and the Gardis. Ram Shastri had met Raghunathrao to record his statement, but could not gather anything significant from him. He spoke to Anandibai also, who feigned ignorance about the incident. Ram Shastri was puzzled that the incident which took place inside the Shaniwar Wada on a busy day had no witnesses who could come forward and speak to him. When he tried to approach the Gardis, no one agreed to talk to him. After a lot of persuasions and on instructions from Raghunathrao, Sumer Singh did give his statement, but he also did not share any valuable information.

Ram Shastri had corroborated the happenings of that day, but could not make any conclusion, though all the statements he had heard so far, were pointing towards only one person.

Parvatibai was in her chamber, waiting for Ram Shastri. She had become the symbol of grit and patience over the years after the death of her husband, Sadashiv Bhau, in Panipat. Parvatibai never accepted the fact that her husband had died and she lived a life of a married woman, despite strong social criticism. When Narayanrao was murdered, she felt guilty and stood like a mother for Gangabai. Parvatibai blamed herself for the murder of Narayanrao and out of guilt, she gave up all the religious and social rituals which she followed even after the death of her husband. It was late in the morning when Ram Shastri reached her chamber and was surprised to see her situation. Unlike on all occasions where she was always well dressed, he found her sitting on a chair in a plain sari which was loosely tucked, her hair was not done properly, and looking at her frail body, he could guess that she had not eaten for days.

"I am bothering you, Vahinisaheb. Forgive me for that."Ram Shastri wished her, he was saddened to see Parvatibai in such a condition.

"Shastribuwa, I have high hopes from you. You are the only one who can show us some light in this dark time." Parvatibai welcomed him and responded.

"I understand your point, Vahinisaheb. I am trying my best in this investigation."

"I am surprised to see that the world can change so much in a few weeks. I have learned how difficult it has been for you to find a witness. I will be happy to be of any assistance in the case." Parvatibai told him.

"I wanted to talk to you about the activities of the day when Shrimant died. It would be good if you share facts with me without any emotions. Only the things which you have seen with your own eyes or heard with your own ears." Ram Shastri requested her as many rumours were floating around and he was interested only in the facts.

"I was here in my chamber that day as it was around noon and was taking rest. It must be past noon time when I heard some noises from downstairs. I did not go out of my room, but within sometime I sensed that there is commotion going on as I could hear people screaming. I was not sure what was happening and thought of going out to check. When I was getting ready to leave, suddenly someone knocked at the back door of my chamber. This was unusual as very few people in the palace are aware of that door," Parvati told him.

Ram Shastri was listening carefully.

"What did you do then?" he asked.

"When I opened the door, Narayan rushed in and I immediately closed the door. He was very scared at that time."

"Was Shrimant hurt then?"

"No, he was not hurt, but he told me that the Gardis had created a ruckus inside the palace and were after his life. I talked to him for some time and comforted him."

"What did you do after that? When did Shrimant leave for his chamber?" Ram Shastri asked.

"I regret the decision I took on that day. When I sensed the danger roaming around the corridors of the palace, I suggested him to go to Dadasaheb for help." Parvati covered her face with her hands and started sobbing. Ram Shastri waited for her to regain her composure.

"Did Shrimant go to Dadasaheb's room?"Ram Shastri continued her questioning.

"If I would have not suggested him to go to Dadasaheb's room, he would have been alive today. I should have asked him to stay with me. I would have sacrificed my life to save his. At least I would have fought for Narayan." Tears were running down her face.

"I understand, Vahinisaheb. But it was quite natural for you to suggest Shrimant to seek help from Dadasaheb."Ram Shastri consoled her.

"Narayan trusted me and, on that day, he left my chamber to go to Dadasaheb's chamber for help. I don't know why I did that. When I think about that day, I feel it was me who took Narayan's life." Parvati was feeling guilty about the advice she gave to Narayanrao. She believed that if she would have asked Narayanrao to stay in her room, no guard would have dared to enter her chamber.

"Did you accompany Shrimant to Dadasaheb's chamber?" Ram Shastri continued.

"No, I didn't go with Narayan. He went in the direction of Dadasaheb's chamber. I had closed the door of my chamber once he left. There was chaos at that time and I could not gauge the situation well ." Parvatibai told him.

"Anything you have heard or seen after that?"

"All I heard was that Narayan was killed in the riots instigated by the Gardis."

"Thank you, Vahinisaheb, for sharing the details of that day."

"What is the conclusion of your investigation, Shastribuwa?"

"I have not concluded anything yet."

"Shastribuwa, the whole Maratha empire knows who is behind Narayan's murder. How come you are not able to conclude?" Parvatibai asked emotionally.

"We all know that Shrimant was murdered in the palace on that day, but I have not seen any proof yet. We all know who is the suspect, but I can't base my judgement on emotions. I need proof. No eye witness is willing to testify, Vahinisaheb." Ram Shastri replied.

The meeting with Parvatibai did confirm that she had asked Narayanrao to go to Raghunathrao and he had followed her instructions. Parvatibai was the last person who had seen him alive and had given a statement to Ram Shastri. All the incidents of that day had been corroborated so far, but without an eyewitness or solid proof, he could not conclude his investigation.

It was late in the evening when Ram Shastri reached home and was talking to Janaki when Gangabai arrived at his house. Gangabai had not ventured out much after the death of her husband and remained confined to her chamber only. Her arrival had been completely unexpected for Ram Shastri.

"Vahinisaheb, why have you come here in such a situation? You could have sent a message and I would have come to meet you," a surprised Ram Shastri asked her.

"I heard that you came to the palace today, but since you did not come to meet me, I thought I will come and meet you here, Shastribuwa." Gangabai replied as she was expecting Ram Shastri to meet her at Shaniwar Wada and give her an update about the investigation.

"I apologize, Vahinisaheb, for not meeting you today. In the interest of all, it would be good if you go to the palace now. I will come and meet you tomorrow."

"I have come for the best interest of all, Shastribuwa. I have come to beg you for help."

"Vahinisaheb, don't insult me by saying that. I am the servant of the Marathas. You just order what I can do for you."

"You do justice, Shastribuwa. Swari was killed behind the walls of the palace. People are talking behind my back about his murder. Some people talk about the murderer. There are rumours, conspiracies, and a threat always looming large. I don't care for my life, but I am worried about the child in my womb. I am not able to sleep in the nights, Shastribuwa." Gangabai was crying.

"Please compose yourself. Such thoughts at this time are not good for you. Please go back to the palace." Janaki came forward and sat near Gangabai.

"I have lost everything, Janaki. There is nothing to go back to in that palace. That palace haunts me," she responded.

"I will come to the palace tomorrow and meet you." Ram Shastri told her again.

Gangabai did not speak for a while. She composed herself, kept one hand on her belly, and got up to leave. When she reached the gate, she turned back. Ram Shastri was looking at her and she was staring through him with a stiff face. It was a heart-wrenching moment for Ram Shastri. He felt ashamed. The empire had stooped so low that the pregnant widow of the Peshwa had to beg for justice. For the first time in his life, Ram Shastri felt ashamed to be the judge of the empire. He could not look into her eyes and lowered his gaze.

"Shastribuwa! You are respected for your knowledge, righteousness, integrity and justice across the empire and in many other parts of the world. If I can't get justice from a person like you, then I would never get justice. Now I will only see you once the justice is delivered." Gangabai challenged Ram Shastri and left his house.

* * *

Kamla was inside Sumer Singh's chamber. They were lying cuddled together in his bed. This had become a regular practice since the day they had met accidentally outside his chamber. Kamla was aware of the weakness of a man and during these encounters with Sumer Singh in his chamber, she had gathered some crucial information about the incident, but the solid proof was still missing which Ram Shastri needed.

"Be with me for some more time. Why are you in a hurry today?" She asked Sumer Singh who got up from the bed and was putting on his clothes.

"I have to go and meet Dadasaheb. Hope I would be paid the promised money today. I am planning to leave Poona forever." Sumer Singh told her.

"Will you leave me here alone? I thought we will be together forever," Kamla said dramatically.

"I will take you with me, my love," Sumer Singh said and kissed her.

Kamla had managed to earn his full trust in the last few weeks. He talked to her freely and shared his secrets with her.

"What if he doesn't give you money? Do you trust such a person?" Kamla asked casually.

"I don't trust anyone in this family Kamla, but I know how to get my money. If Dadasaheb will try to act smart with me, I will make the proof against him public. Then the whole world will know who had ordered the murder of Narayanrao," Sumer Singh spoke in an arrogant tone.

"What proof are you talking about? Did Dadasaheb give you orders to kill Narayanrao in writing?" Kamla continued the discussion.

"Yes. In writing on a paper with a signature and the royal seal of Dadasaheb!" replied Sumer Singh.

Kamla's mind was running with all the possibilities. This was the proof Ram Shastri was talking about and this was the proof for which she had to get into bed with a man like Sumer Singh.

"You are a very smart man, Sumer. You have a powerful weapon against the most powerful person in the Maratha empire. I would be happy to spend the rest of my life with you. I would like to hold that order in my hands which gives you so much power." She hugged him from behind.

Kamla was not educated and could not read much. Neither she could recognize the royal seal. However, the confidence in Sumer Singh's voice confirmed to her that he was not lying.

"You want to see that order? Let me show you then." Sumer Singh removed an iron barrel from the floor and moved the two wooden planks. Below that in a long metal box, he had hidden his secret. The secret which could change the future of the Maratha empire if it falls into the right hands. An uneducated batik was trying to do what the educated and powerful could not. She was fighting for the person who had fought for her.

Kamla looked at the paper, puzzled. She could not understand anything from it. She did not show any emotions and casually handed it back to Sumer Singh who kept it back at the same place and then went out to meet Raghunathrao.

Kamla walked out of the chamber, all the guards on duty were looking at her. She was a prostitute for them who came to their master to satisfy his sexual desires. Kamla walked away in the way a prostitute should walk, with a swag. She knew guards would be looking at her as she passed in front of them. Her movements were in rhythm with her bosom. The guards were staring at her as she passed them. They were drooping.

She had played her role with perfection. For the guards, she was nothing more than a prostitute, they would not be suspicious of her anymore. As she came close to Gangabai's chamber, she rushed in.

Bhavanrao was waiting for Sumer Singh outside the camp of Raghunathrao. Sumer Singh was not in a good mood. The money and the forts which were promised to him were only promises and had not materialized for him.

"Dadasaheb, I have delivered my promise to you, but I am still waiting for my reward," Sumer Singh told Raghunathrao.

"Sumer Singh, we will settle all your dues today. Don't worry about that." Raghunathrao replied, but Sumer did not trust him and when he heard this, he did not react. Raghunathrao signalled Bhavanrao who was ready with the money wrapped inside a cloth. Bhavanrao opened the wrap and showed it to Sumer Singh. He had a broad smile on his face.

When Visaji Krishna returned from the North and met Raghunathrao, he was carrying cash collected as revenue from various kingdoms on the way along with some jewellery. Raghunathrao did not allow him to deposit any of that in the royal treasury and seized all of it. It gave a huge relief to cash-deprived Raghunathrao who settled the dues with the Gardis.

"We have also delivered on our promise, Sumer Singh. You will be the in-charge of security for our coronation." Raghunathrao ordered.

"Sarkar, I will be honoured"' Sumer Singh thanked Raghunathrao and came out of the tent. While walking out, he overheard the discussion between Bhavanrao and Raghunathrao, they were talking about Gangabai. Sumer Singh did not pay heed to the discussion. He had heard the rumours earlier, but he did not want to be a part of any more conspiracies.

* * *

Anandibai had made plans to strike, again. Tuloji was in her chamber when Khadak Singh arrived.

"Swari will become Peshwa very soon, Khadak Singh. The Gardis will be rewarded for the work you have delivered." Anandibai told Khadak Singh.

"Sarkar, you are very generous," Khadak Singh replied.

"You have to complete one more task for me, Khadak Singh," Anandibai spoke calmly.

"Hukum, Sarkar." Khadak Singh was worried that this time he was invited alone and Sumer Singh was not involved in this task.

"This task and the reward wili be only for you, Khadak Singh. I trust that you would keep it to yourself." Anandibai was trying to lure him with the money.

"I will follow the order, Sarkar." Khadak Singh nodded in affirmation.

"Gangabai should also meet the same fate as her husband. You would be rewarded with one lakh rupees in cash for the task, Khadak Singh," Anandibai told him.

Khadak Singh remained silent for a while. It was not the first time he was hearing this. There were whispers across Shaniwar Wada about the threat to the life of Gangabai. Sumer Singh had talked to all the Gardis and had already given his verdict on this subject.

"Sarkar, forgive me, please. I can't do this task. Harming a pregnant widow is against our values." Khadak Singh refused to accept the order given by Anandibai.

"Khadak Singh, you are disobeying an order from the Peshwa." Tuloji tried to force him.

"Sarkar, if you want you can put me in jail or kill me, but I won't do this for any reward." Khadak Singh stood firm on his decision.

Khadak Singh was standing in front of Anandibai with his head hung low. She was contemplating her next step, but there was nothing she could do without the Gardis.

"You can leave." Anandibai ordered and banged her hand on the pillar of her chamber in frustration.

'Gardis would not do this task,' concluded Anandibai.

16 CORONATION OF THE NEW PESHWA

Sakharam Bapu was at his house alone, thinking about the events of the last few weeks. He had given all his life to the empire and played a vital role in administrative affairs at the capital palace and planned various war campaigns for many decades. When he gained consciousness, he realized his mistake of being a blind supporter of Raghunathrao. As the power in the empire had slowly shifted, Sakharam Bapu gauged the situation carefully and vowed to correct his mistakes.

Bapu, being a well-connected and experienced leader, knew about the activities of both the factions, but no one had any idea what he had on his mind. The palanquin had arrived at his gate and a servant came calling for him.

Sakharam Bapu and Nana Phadnis had been part of the Maratha empire for long and he knew that it won't be easy to convince Nana at that time. Ram Shastri could trust him, but he decided to meet him later. The first step in his plan was to meet Raghunathrao, who was still camping on the outskirts of Poona and had not shifted back to Shaniwar Wada. As he was a known supporter of Raghunathrao, he decided to play his cards accordingly.

"Bapu, we cannot change the past, but we have to plan for the future. We have lost Narayan and I am left with no choice, but to manage the affairs of the state," Raghunathrao told him after pleasantries as both of them were talking in private at Raghunathrao's camp.

"You are right, Dadasaheb. The affairs of the state should be managed. I have learned that Nizam is gathering his forces to attack our territories. He wants to take benefit of the turmoil here in Poona," Bapu responded calmly. He was choosing his words very carefully and observing the reaction of Raghunathrao.

"There are many enemies who would be waiting for the right opportunity. I am also worried about the external threats at this time, Bapu. I am planning a campaign against Nizam. What do you suggest?" Raghunathrao asked him. Raghunathrao always trusted Sakharam Bapu and when Bapu realized that Raghunathrao still trusted him, he decided to play along.

"You have to formally take charge, Dadasaheb, and then go on a campaign. I suggest that you immediately send someone to Satara to get the robes of Peshwa and then start your campaign against Nizam. Some people are very upset about the incident at Shaniwar Wada so it is better that instead of you, someone else goes to get robes of Peshwa. You start your campaign and that way you would get sympathy from the public too." Bapu thought for a while before sharing his opinion with Raghunathrao. It was a well-calculated move, but could have gone either way.

Raghunathrao thought about the suggestion and it made perfect sense to him. He would excuse himself and instead, send his son to Satara and move on a campaign against Nizam. This would send a positive message about him across the empire. But if he would be on the campaign, it would delay his coronation ceremony. It has been a tradition that the coronation ceremony of the new Peshwa takes place at the Ganpati Rang Mahal of Shaniwar Wada.

"Once the robes of the Peshwa arrive for you, the coronation ceremony can be arranged somewhere on your route. Dadasaheb, in the current scenario, it is better if your coronation takes place somewhere else instead of Shaniwar Wada." Sensing that Raghunathrao was in dilemma about the coronation, Bapu gave him a pragmatic suggestion.

Raghunathrao was impressed by the advice of Sakharam Bapu, who came out of the chamber and boarded his palanquin. It was a successful meeting for him as Raghunathrao would move away from the Maratha capital.

A few days later, Raghunathrao gathered the troops to go on a campaign against Nizam. Amritrao was sent to Satara to meet the figurehead Chhatrapati and collect robes of Peshwa for his father.

* * *

On one side, Raghunathrao and his group of loyalists were planning the coronation ceremony and on the other side, Nana Phadnis was planning a revolution against the would-be-Peshwa. Both the groups were concerned about the progress in the investigation of Ram Shastri.

"Shastribuwa, Dadasaheb has already sent Amritrao to Satara to get the robes of Peshwa. Soon, he will officially take the charge of Peshwai. Now the future of the empire depends on the outcome of your investigation," Nana Phadnis was talking to Ram Shastri.

"My investigation so far points to one person only, but I am yet to get concrete evidence to conclude my investigation and pass a judgement." Ram Shastri sounded dejected.

"I understand, Shastribuwa. Your judgement would have long-term consequences on the empire and its future." Nana Phadnis consoled him.

"I hope I will be able to conclude my investigation soon. I am also worried about the safety of Gangabai."

"We have alerted Vahinisaheb, but I understand your concern. We are planning to move her to Purandar soon. Haripant will ensure her transit from Poona to Purandar and then Naroji would take care of her security at Purandar." Nana Phadnis told him the details.

"Her safety is of paramount importance, Nana. I know that you are busy with political activities, but she would be the key to any activity you plan in the future."

"Yes, Shastribuwa. I have faulted once. I will not repeat the same mistake. I will personally ensure her safety and take care of her movement from Poona to Purandar."

"I also wanted to speak to you about Sakharam Bapu." Ram Shastri broached the sensitive topic he wanted to discuss. Nana Phadnis and Sakharam Bapu had always been adversaries while both of them held senior posts in the Maratha empire.

"How is he now? I could not check on him after that incident at Parvati temple where the pandit found him on that day." Nana asked casually.

"Bapu is doing good now. He is slowly recovering. When I met him, he was deeply disturbed by the incident. He has been regretting that he could not do anything to prevent the tragic incident."

"He always supported Dadasaheb, not sure if he was part of the plan or not. It is not easy to trust him, Shastribuwa," Nana

Phadnis shared his concern even before Ram Shastri could speak anything in support of Sakharam Bapu.

"I know, Nana. It won't be easy for you to trust Bapu. I suggest you go and meet him once. Talk to him at length. He would be a big help in your political revolution. Don't forget his political wisdom and the respect he commands from many allies. I suggest that you continue your work as usual." Ram Shastri told him.

The murder of Narayanrao had created a political vacuum in the Maratha empire. Nana Phadnis and other senior ministers felt that Raghunathrao was not suitable for the post of Peshwa and his suspected involvement in the murder of Narayanrao had dented his image. When Nana floated the idea of a parallel political force against Raghunathrao, he had decided to keep it to only a small group. The key members of the group were Trimbakrao, Haripant Phadke, and him. On a few occasions, he had taken advice from Ram Shastri as the support of the chief justice of the empire would be the key to any political alternative.

As the idea of a parallel political force was taking shape, Raghunathrao was also strengthening his grip on the power. Raghunathrao officially declared himself as the next Peshwa and the date of coronation was also announced. Alegaon was chosen as the venue for the coronation of Raghunathrao.

Raghunathrao was on a campaign at that time and had reached Alegaon to set the camp there. Amritrao was advised to come to Alegaon directly from Satara. Anandibai arrived a few days later and once the robes of Peshwa were received from Satara, preparation for the coronation started in full swing.

Alegaon was a smaller town compared to Poona. Fortunately, the town had a big hall which was chosen as the venue for the coronation. Anandibai was personally leading all the preparations; after all, her dream was about to materialize.

The venue was decorated exactly like the Ganpati Rang Mahal of Shaniwar Wada and its entrance was designed like the Ganesh Darwaza. Seating arrangements were made for all the dignitaries of the Maratha empire and the musnud was also prepared exactly like the one inside the Ganpati Rang Mahal. All the dignitaries were invited to attend the coronation ceremony of the new Peshwa.

Nana Phadnis was at his house when he received the invitation. He already had all the information about the coronation ceremony and had decided to attend the ceremony along with other senior ministers. The investigation into the murder of Narayanrao was still inconclusive, so he called on Haripant Phadke and Trimbakrao and together, they went to meet Ram Shastri.

"It is unfortunate to witness what is about to happen, but there is little we could do now, Shastribuwa. We have decided to be a part of the coronation ceremony," Nana spoke first.

"I agree with you, Nana, you should go and join the ceremony," responded Ram Shastri.

"There are still five days left for the ceremony, but we would be leaving tomorrow morning. It would be convenient for all of us if you too travel with us," Nana requested him.

"I will not join the coronation ceremony, Nana," Ram Shastri responded thoughtfully.

"Shastribuwa, you suggested us to go about our work as normal and now you won't be joining the ceremony? You have a very important role to play in it." Nana was surprised to hear his decision.

"Managing the political activities is very different than managing judicial activities, Nana. I know I advised you to do your work, as usual, that way you would stay closer to the centre of power and have all the information," Ram Shastri replied.

"Your absence in the ceremony could create many issues, Shastribuwa. If you are not there, Dadasaheb would treat it as an open revolt against him," Nana was concerned about Ram Shastri.

"I am not concerned about that, Nana. Even if he removes me from the post of judge, I am okay. But my conscience doesn't allow me to be a part of this coronation ceremony."

"As you suggest, Shastribuwa. We will be leaving tomorrow morning."

After Nana, Trimbakrao, and Haripant left, Ram Shastri looked at the invitation letter which had arrived a day earlier. It had the signature and royal seal of Raghunathrao.

Despite being the judge of the Maratha empire, he had no powers. He could not deliver justice for Narayanrao and his widow. Ram Shastri was pained.

* * *

Kamla would spend hours daily in Sumer Singh's chamber, even if he was not there. She would walk into his chamber and wait for his arrival. She had meticulously studied his routine, his habits, and sleeping patterns and mapped his trusted security guards. There had been days when Sumer would not arrive and she would return to servant quarters without meeting him. Guards on duty would get seductive looks from her.

Kamla carefully observed everything inside the chamber and on two occasions she had taken out the paper from the metal box which was hidden under the wooden planks, stared at it, and kept it back. A day before Sumer Singh left for Alegaon after he was made security in-charge of the coronation ceremony, Kamla did check the paper. It was at the same place.

"You can't even live for a day without..." the guard on the duty commented lustfully. She responded with a flirtatious smile and entered the chamber of Sumer Singh.

She had made many trips to the chamber in last few days and on all these occasions, she had stood close to the door and listened to the movement outside. She had planned it well. The most trusted guard of Sumer Singh was not on duty and the new guard would not dare to question or frisk the mistress of his master.

This was the moment.

She went inside the chamber, closed the door, and waited for a while. When nothing untoward happened, she slowly removed the wooden plank and took out the metal box. The paper she was looking for was still there. Kamla carefully kept the similar-looking paper in the metal box and hid the stolen paper under her saree. After replacing the paper and keeping the box back in its place, she waited for some more time to relax her nerves and once she sensed the right opportunity, she left the chamber.

The guards on the duty smiled again. She too responded with a seductive smile on her face.

'*Bitch,*' thought the guards.

'*Idiots,*' thought Kamla.

* * *

Ram Shastri had not ventured out of his house after his meeting with Nana. His body was burning with high temperature and his face had lost its charm. There was sadness in his eyes. Janaki came with his dinner and helped him to sit.

"You have not eaten anything for two days. You should eat something now," Janaki requested him.

"It is better to die of hunger, Janaki, than to die of shame. I am concerned about the activities of the empire, Janaki..."

"If you are confident about the culprit, why don't you go and announce the judgement?" Janaki questioned his stand.

"I could have done that, Janaki, but if there would have been concrete proof. It won't be easy to question the would-be Peshwa in the court without proof."

"What has happened and whatever is happening is beyond your control. I know you have done your best, but if power and greed take such a shape, no one can do anything!"

"I am saddened that now there is not much of a difference between the Mughals and the Marathas. Might is right even in the Maratha empire now."

"If you will stay hungry like this, you won't be able to do anything. Let me get some water for you." Janaki told him and got up to fetch water. As she was filling the water from the pitcher, there was a knock on the door.

"Shastribuwa, Shastribuwa..." someone was frantically shouting at his door. Janaki rushed to open the door.

"Kamla?" Janaki looked at her, surprised.

"Where is Shastribuwa?" Kamla was out of breath when she reached their home and sat on the floor near Ram Shastri.

"Kamla, what happened?" He was barely able to speak.

"Shastribuwa, you told me that to deliver justice for Shrimant, you need some proof. For the last few weeks, I was trying to get the proof for you."

"Yes, Kamla. I still do not have any concrete proof." Ram Shastri responded meekly.

"I have..." Kamla took out the paper she was carrying and handed it to Ram Shastri.

Janaki brought the lamp closer to them. Ram Shastri was still not interested in the paper. He had no inklings of what Kamla had handed to him.

"What is this, Kamla?" asked Ram Shastri.

"I can't read, Shastribuwa, you can. Check yourself and do tell me whether my efforts have been successful or not?" Kamla asked eagerly.

Ram Shastri signalled Janaki to bring the lamp further close to him as he slowly opened the paper. When he finished reading it, he stood up from his bed. There was a glow on his face which was visible in the light of the lamp. He no more looked tired. It seemed a miracle had happened and Ram Shastri had gained his composure and his energy was back.

"Where did you get this, Kamla?" Ram Shastri asked.

"I have stolen this from Sumer Singh's chamber. Tell me, Shastribuwa, will it help?" Kamla asked.

"You have done a remarkable service for the empire, Kamla. What the Chief Justice of this empire could not do, you have done it."He took the paper in his hands and bowed in front of Kamla to pay respect to the batik who had sacrificed her honour for justice. In his eyes, her place was higher than that of a judge.

"Even if I am caught or killed now, I have no fears, Shastribuwa."

"You are under my protection, Kamla. No one would be able to touch you," Ram Shastri said with confidence.

"What is there in this paper?" Janaki was pleasantly surprised by the sudden demeanour change of her husband and asked him.

"The future of Maratha empire," Ram Shastri spoke with confidence now and enquired some more details from Kamla who told him everything about her activities in the last few weeks. The more Ram Shastri heard her, the more his respect grew for the batik.

"I have to leave for Alegaon tomorrow morning." Ram Shastri told Janaki once the discussion was over and rushed out of his house.

"But where are you going now?" Janaki asked him when he was rushing out of his house. He no more cared about food or fever.

"To arrange travel for tomorrow!" Ram Shastri left his house to make the travel arrangements. He had planned to leave for Alegaon early morning and for the travel, he not only needed the palanquin, but also some armed troops in case of any skirmishes on the way.

He had the proof under his arm and the judgement on his mind. The coronation of the new Peshwa was still two days away.

17 THE JUDGEMENT DAY

October 1773
Maratha Darbar, Alegaon

"Sumer Singh, Khadak Singh and other Gardis have killed Narayan," Raghunathrao spoke the truth finally Sumer Singh was stunned to hear his name in full darbar. Ram Shastri looked around the darbar and waited for everyone to digest the shocking truth they had just heard. Slowly, he turned to face Sumer Singh.

"Sumer Singh?" Ram Shastri asked Raghunathrao, pointing his hand towards him. Raghunathrao nodded his head in affirmation. Ram Shastri intentionally spoke his name in a loud voice so that everyone in the darbar could hear it clearly.

"The person who had killed Shrimant Narayanrao is part of your coronation ceremony? It is your duty to punish the murderer, Dadasaheb. But what I am seeing here is that you are rewarding him," Ram Shastri again questioned Raghunathrao.

"If Sumer Singh and Khadak Singh had killed Shrimant, why are they still alive and why have they been given the responsibility of managing the security of the new Peshwa?" Ram Shastri asked again, this time he was mainly addressing the darbar and making his point clear. He was slowly peeling off the conspiracy which was being hatched behind the four walls of Shaniwar Wada and he was headed for its climax.

The guilt was so heavy that Raghunathrao was not able to speak anything, his head hung low with shame.

"I know, Dadasaheb, it would be difficult for you to answer this question, but I can answer this on your behalf," Ram Shastri continued to come to the last part of his investigation.

A few weeks in the future...

The idea of a parallel government was taking concrete shape. Nana Phadnis had initiated secret discussions with many Maratha chiefs and loyalists. There were only three members initially and Ram Shastri was kept in the loop. Nana Phadnis secretly communicated with Parvatibai, who extended full support to the revolution to protect the honour of the Peshwa family and to bring the murderer of Narayanrao to justice. Parvatibai decided to lead all the communication related to the revolution and wrote personal letters to many Maratha chiefs. These letters explained the tragedy in detail and had the royal seal of Narayanrao's widow, Gangabai, to garner sympathy for both, her, and her unborn child.

"Shastribuwa, the Gardis were upset with their salary payment." Anandibai tried to intervene, but Ram Shastri lifted his index finger and signalled her to stop. He conveyed to her that she could not play any more games.

"On that day Shaniwar Wada witnessed all the gravest sins mentioned in Hindu texts – ***bal hatya, brahman hatya, stree hatya*** and ***gau hatya.*** Shaniwar Wada has been polluted forever, Dadasaheb. This event would always be remembered in Maratha's history. The future generations will never forgive us, Dadasaheb. Today you are telling this darbar that all this had been executed by Sumer Singh and some other Gardis. Such a sin was committed by Gardis just because they did not get their salaries on time? My investigation tells me a different story, Dadasaheb. Sumer Singh just followed the orders to kill Shrimant Narayanrao, the orders which were issued by you." Ram Shastri made a statement that stunned everyone in the darbar. Sumer Singh and the Gardis could not tolerate it anymore.

Swords were raised from the camp of Raghunathrao again. Sumer Singh with his team of Gardis tried to attack Ram Shastri and surrounded Raghunathrao to protect him. Mahadji Scindia and Haripant Phadke had their troops with them. They quickly formed a circle around Ram Shastri to protect him.

The great Maratha empire stood divided into two factions, both sides ready to attack. Standing fearlessly between them, Ram Shastri was fighting for the truth, for justice.

Ram Shastri was pained to see the proceedings in the darbar. The Marathas who had ruled from North to South had swords raised in their court and were fighting for the throne. There had been numerous incidents in Hindustan and in the world when power had been snatched by deception, conspiracy or murder, but that had never happened in the history of the Maratha empire.

It was an emotional moment for Ram Shastri who had huge respect for Madhavrao Peshwa, but could not keep his promise to him. At that moment in court, it was difficult for him to control his emotions. It would have been such a different scenario had Madhavrao Peshwa been here. No one would have dared to raise a sword in the darbar. No one would have dared to speak against Ram Shastri, against the eminent judge and his judgement. The judgement would have been delivered fearlessly and had been acted as per the rules.

A few weeks in the future.

Nana Phadnis devoted himself to the cause of the revolution to save the Maratha empire and for some time, all the activities of the revolution were done in secrecy. When the revolution had significant support, a group of twelve members was formed to run the government. This group was called the 'Barbhai council'. The eleven members of the group were Nana Phadnis, Trimbakrao Pethe, Haripant Phadke, Naro Appaji, Apaji Balwant, Anandrao Panse, Baburao Keshav, Krishnaji Bahirao Thate, Anand Rao Jiwaji, Visaji Krishna Biniwale and Apaji Prandare. Parvatibai moved the first proposal of the council which was to bring Raghunathrao to justice and the proposal was accepted by all members. It was Trimbakrao who suggested that Sakharam Bapu be made a part of the revolution. Some members had doubts, but the proposal was accepted. Thus, the twelve member group which became popular as the Barbhai council initiated the process to form a republic government in Poona.

As a judge, Ram Shastri had to control his emotions. Justice is not based on emotions. It is based on facts and evidence. In any way, he couldn't allow his emotions to impact his judgement. He couldn't deliver a judgement that would be called emotional or based on feelings and rumours. His judgement would be purely based on facts and proof.

"I did not kill Narayan. I did not kill him." Raghunathrao pleaded in the darbar and sat on the floor in front of the musnud.

"Shastribuwa, do you have any proof to support your baseless allegation?" Anandibai stood up and questioned him. She had assumed that Ram Shastri was playing with emotions and guilt and had no concrete evidence against Raghunathrao.

"When the riots broke out in Shaniwar Wada, Shrimant was scared for his life and he ran to Parvatibai for help. She suggested to Shrimant to go to Dadasaheb. When he came out of her chamber, the Gardis were running behind him for his life. Shrimant ran to the chamber of Dadasaheb shouting, *kaka mala vachva.* Shrimant trusted you, Dadasaheb, and came to you for help. What did you do? You betrayed Shrimant. You betrayed Madhavrao Peshwa. You betrayed the whole Maratha empire, Dadasaheb. You have disgraced the legacy of your father, the great Bajirao Peshwa. On what basis do you want to become Peshwa? You have killed your own son, Dadasaheb."

Ram Shastri was unstoppable in the court. He had got the opportunity to deliver justice and he wanted to leave no stone unturned. He intended to kill all the sympathy and support for Raghunathrao in the Maratha empire.

"Shastribuwa, do you have any credible proof other than these unfounded statements?" Anandibai asked again. Ram Shastri looked towards her and took out a paper from his bag and started reading it.

Anandibai's face turned pale when she looked at the paper that Ram Shastri had in his hands.

"Sumer Singh! You are ordered to kill Narayanrao. For this work, you will be paid three lacs in cash and the fort of Purandar. Signed by Raghunathrao with his royal seal." Ram Shastri read the paper for everyone in the darbar. He then handed it to Haripant who thereafter passed it to Mahadji Scindia.

"I did not order to kill Narayan. I ordered to capture." He looked towards Anandibai, who was sitting on the first floor.

Raghunathrao was speaking the truth. He had been eyeing the post of the Peshwa for over a decade and finally planned to snatch it by imprisoning Narayanrao. The plan which was hatched by him was just to capture Narayanrao, put him under house arrest, and take the Peshwai. Anandibai, on the other hand, had made her own plans.

She had known that change of power by force had never happened in the Maratha empire and even if Raghunathrao would succeed in snatching the power by imprisoning Narayanrao, he would not be able to hold onto it. Many powerful ministers did not support Raghunathrao and they could gather support and revolt. Worst case, they could even do the same to Raghunathrao as he had thought to do with Narayanrao.

Anandibai had not shared her plan with Raghunathrao, who wrote a letter and ordered Sumer Singh to capture, *dharaava*, Narayanrao. The letter was written in Marathi and had the royal seal of Raghunathrao and his signature. He naively passed the letter to Anandibai. As the ink on the letter was still fresh,

Anandibai decided to execute her plan, the plan that would be remembered forever in Maratha history. If Raghunathrao wanted to be Peshwa and hold onto the Peshwai, Narayanrao had to be removed forever. Anandibai knew that there was no other way. She went to her chamber with pen, ink, and that paper. She read the paper again and decided to change one letter in that paper.

She picked the paper and changed *dha* to *ma* and the order now said *maraava,* which meant to kill Narayanrao. Then she handed over the order to Sumer Singh Gardi. Raghunathrao never got a chance to see that letter again. He was betrayed by his wife.

A few weeks in the future.

As Raghunathrao was consolidating his position, Nana Phadnis, Parvatibai, and other Barbhai members were garnering support for the revolution. The revolution was declared public and on the 30th of January 1774 – the Barbhai council declared itself as the parallel government in Poona. Special agents were appointed to go to each village and explain the objective of the Barbhai council, Parvatibai personally met many Maratha Chiefs and royals. There was discomfort across the empire about the way power had shifted in Poona and a personal appeal from Parvatibai and Gangabai had created a sympathy wave. But sympathy was not enough to stop Raghunathrao, who had learned about the Barbhai council and had started his march towards Poona to assert his power and take control of Shaniwar Wada. The bugle for the civil war had been sounded.

The Barbhai council had its biggest task at hand, to garner military support and stop Raghunathrao.

"Narayan has left us, Shastribuwa. This happened in my presence. I could not save Narayan. I am a culprit, Shastribuwa..." Raghunathrao finally spoke, he had guilt all over his face.

"I am happy that you have accepted your sin, Dadasaheb," Ram Shastri was elated to see that Raghunathrao had accepted his crime.

"You are a learned person, Shastribuwa. You can help me pay for my sins. Help me, Shastribuwa. Tell me, is there any penance for such a sin, Shastribuwa?"

"There is penance for every sin, Dadasaheb."

"Please tell me, Shastribuwa. And I will follow your command." Raghunathrao got up from the floor, walked and stood near Ram Shastri. He was keen to hear the punishment for his sins.

"For such a heinous crime and betrayal of trust, there is only one penance, Dadasaheb." Ram Shastri was getting ready for the last blow to Raghunathrao.

"I would be happy to follow your order, Shastribuwa," Raghunathrao declared in the darbar.

The darbar, which represented a battlefield with swords raised from both sides, was looking towards Ram Shastri for an answer. He looked towards helpless Raghunathrao and at all the dignitaries, thinking about the ramifications the judgement could have on the empire. It was a tense moment in the darbar.

Ram Shastri controlled his emotions and tears. It was the most difficult moment of his life and he was worried about whether he would be able to speak and deliver justice.

He closed his eyes, took a deep breath, and cleared his throat. The images of Nanasaheb, Madhavrao, Narayanrao, Gangabai, and other Maratha leaders were in front of his eyes. All of them wanted him to be fearless and honest. He saw the smiling face of Janaki who was telling him to perform his duty for the empire.

"Shastribuwa, I request you to please announce your judgement to the darbar." Mahadji Scindia requested Ram Shastri.

A few weeks in the future.

It was pertinent for the Barbhai council to have the military might to survive and fight against Raghunathrao and other enemies. The Barbhai council members reached out to many allies to garner armed support for the Barbhai government. Nana Phadnis reached out to Sabaji Bhosale for support and promised him that he would be recognized as the sena-saheb-subha of Nagpur. Sabaji extended full support to Barbhai government and dispatched the troops from Nagpur to Poona to counter Raghunathrao.

Madhavrao had developed strong relations with Nizam Ali and Nana Phadnis was aware of the bonhomie between the two. Nizam Ali was a tricky ally as he had also enjoyed good relations with Raghunathrao in the past. Nana Phadnis reached out to Nizam Ali for support and to his surprise, Nizam Ali was disgruntled with Raghunathrao and extended full support to the Barbhai government.

The military support was garnered, but officially Raghunathrao was still the Peshwa and any action against him would be equivalent to treason. There was a need for diplomacy and Nana Phadnis played his masterstroke here.

"On that day in Shaniwar Wada, eleven people were murdered and a cow was slaughtered. These are cold-blooded murders that were well planned. I have found forty-nine culprits involved in the crime. In these forty-nine culprits, there were thirteen Gardis, twenty-six brahmins, seven Marathas, and three Prabhus. All these murders were planned and executed under the guidance of Dadasaheb. The penance for such a crime is death." Ram Shastri stopped and took a breath.

"In the murder of Shrimant Narayanrao Peshwa and ten others, I have found that Raghunathrao Bhat had been the key conspirator and I announce death sentence for him as the punishment for his crime. The punishment for others would follow." Ram Shastri announced the judgement in the darbar.

There were murmurs across the darbar. It was shocking for Raghunathrao and Anandibai the way things had turned. Nana Phadnis and Haripant were looking at each other, unable to believe what Ram Shastri had just done.

"Shastribuwa, we respect your judgement, but think about the consequences if this punishment is executed. Dadasaheb is the only heir in the Peshwa family." Mahadji Scindia came forward and spoke.

"Justice is not influenced by its consequences. Justice is delivered for the sin irrespective of the standing of the person in the society. I believe if those in power, those who are the custodian of justice do not respect it, then the public at large would never respect the judgement. I have given deep thought to my judgement and done a thorough investigation. My judgement would remain unchanged, irrespective of its consequences to the empire." Ram Shastri declared.

It became a difficult situation for everyone present in the court. There were murmurs across. Nana was happy at the turn of events, but he could not do anything. Raghunathrao had a large contingent of armed troops with him in Alegaon. Nana and Haripant decided to closely observe the activities of the darbar. The dignitaries were disturbed by the judgement, the political continuity for the empire was more important than justice at that moment.

Anandibai was furious at the judgement and she decided to use force. She signalled Sumer Singh who came forward and spoke to Visajipant. Visajipant held the hand of Raghunathrao and together they walked towards to musnud.

"If the ruler himself is a murderer, you can't expect justice in such an empire. Today in this darbar I resign as the Chief Justice of Maratha empire and leaving this darbar forever."

After saying this, Ram Shastri walked out of the darbar.

* * *

"Shastribuwa, this empire needs you more than ever. If you would leave the empire at such a time, who would deliver justice?" said Trimbakrao who had come to meet Ram Shastri along with Sakharam Bapu, Nana Phadnis, and Haripant Phadke.

"I have delivered my judgement, Nana. There is no point in being the judge if my judgements are not followed."

"Your judgement would be followed, but it needs some time."

"I would be back in Poona when that time comes. I can't go back on my decision, Bapu."

"You are right, Shastribuwa. If an empire can't respect its judge, then it doesn't deserve to have him in-charge. If those who are responsible for the safety and security of everyone breach the trust and kill their loved ones, no one would ever trust the Peshwa. Today I promise you, Shastribuwa, that I will ensure that your judgement is executed. You are leaving Poona, but I will ensure that Raghunathrao can never enter Poona and Shaniwar Wada. I will come and meet you only when this empire is ruled by the right people." Nana spoke passionately.

They wished him luck and together came out of Ram Shastri's house.

It was an emotional moment for Ram Shastri. His heart was filled with gratitude for the support he had received from the senior Maratha ministers and the respect he had received from the people of the empire.

A crowd had gathered outside the house of Ram Shastri. The news about his judgement had reached the city. People were pouring in from all parts of the Maratha empire to get a glimpse of a judge who had sentenced his Peshwa to death. Rumours had already been circulating for weeks, but the judgement of Ram Shastri confirmed that Raghunathrao was the key conspirator in the murder of Narayanrao.

Ram Shastri was ready to leave Poona forever. A bullock cart was waiting for him outside. He thanked everyone gathered there with folded hands. With his family, he boarded the bullock cart.

He remembered the day he had come back from Kashi and joined as a clerk at Shaniwar Wada. He had come a long way since then and his name had become a synonym with justice not only in the Maratha empire, but in many other parts of the world.

Slowly the cart started moving and the crowd followed his cart for a while. People were chanting his name, hail *Nyay Murti* Ram Shastri Prabhune. People kept chanting his name till the time the bullock cart disappeared on the horizon.

Ram Shastri Prabhune became immortal on that day.

A few weeks in the future.

Sakharam Bapu and Nana Phadnis went to Satara to meet the Chhatrapati Ram Raje. It was Chhatrapati who officially decided on the successor to the Peshwai. Nana Phadnis put forward his point about the injustice done to Narayanrao and Gangabai, explaining to Ram Raje about the incident. Nana Phadnis was also carrying the letters written by Parvatibai along with the royal seal of Gangabai. Ram Shastri had also written to Ram Raje and shared all the details of his investigation into the murder. He had also suggested that it would not be right for the empire if Raghunathrao continued as the Peshwa.

On 17 February 1774, the Chhatrapati came out with a proclamation that declared the Peshwai of Raghunathrao null and void. Chhatrapati also asked people to support the armies of the Barbhai council against Raghunathrao. In less than four months after taking charge, Raghunathrao was officially removed from the post of Peshwa and he became a fugitive for life.

On the 18th April, 1774, Gangabai gave birth to a son who was named Sawai Madhavrao. A few weeks after his birth, he became the youngest Peshwa ever and Barbhai council officially governed the Maratha empire.